Vicky

"You Know," ...
"Maybe I'm Not The Only ...
Who Has Some Facing Up To Do."

"What's that supposed to mean?" Alicia asked.

"That maybe it's time you face a few fears of your own. Like the fear that I don't really love you, that you're not pretty enough to love, that I must have some ulterior motive for loving you. Loving someone means trusting them."

"Exactly. And did you trust me when you didn't tell me about your past?"

"Is this your way of repaying me for that?"

"No!" Alicia bit back her tears. How could they be so close and still misunderstand each other so greatly? It felt as if there were a gulf between them as wide as the Grand Canyon. "You'd better go. You'll miss your flight."

"I'll be back."

"Don't make promises you can't keep."

He glared at her. "I'll be back."

Dear Reader:

Welcome to Silhouette Desire – provocative, compelling, contemporary love stories written by and for today's woman. These are stories to treasure.

Each and every Silhouette Desire is a wonderful romance in which the emotional and the sensual go hand in hand. When you open a Desire, you enter a whole new world – a world that has, naturally, a perfect hero just waiting to whisk you away! A Silhouette Desire can be light-hearted or serious, but it will always be satisfying.

We hope you enjoy this Desire today – and will go on to enjoy many more.

Please write to us:

Jane Nicholls
Silhouctte Books
PO Box 236
Thornton Road
Croydon
Surrey
CR9 3RU

CATHIE LINZ

HANDYMAN

Silhouette Desire

Originally Published by Silhouette Books
a division of
Harlequin Enterprises Ltd.

*First published in Great Britain in 1991
by Silhouette Books, Eton House, 18-24 Paradise Road,
Richmond, Surrey TW9 1SR*

© Cathie L. Baumgardner 1991

Silhouette, Silhouette Desire and Colophon are
Trade Marks of Harlequin Enterprises B.V.

ISBN 0 373 58189 0

22 – 9106

Made and printed in Great Britain

CATHIE LINZ

was in her mid-twenties when she left her career in a university law library to become a full-time writer of contemporary romance fiction. Since then, this Chicago author has had several books published. She enjoys hearing from readers and has received fan mail from as far away as Nigeria!

An avid world traveler, Cathie got the idea for *Handyman* during a recent visit to the Canadian Rockies, which quickly became one of her favorite places. After exploring the beautiful scenery, she headed home to her two cats, her trusty word processor and her hidden cache of Oreo cookies!

Other Silhouette Books by Cathie Linz

Silhouette Desire

Change of Heart
A Friend in Need
As Good as Gold
Adam's Way
Smiles

For my editor,
Jackie Brilliant,
who gave me
the best things an editor
can give a writer—
freedom, encouragement, and friendship.
Best of luck in your new life!

One

"These your bags?"

Alicia Donnelly nodded at the man's curt question, but otherwise didn't pay much attention to him. She was too busy searching the crowd for her father's friendly face. Her flight from Minneapolis to Calgary had landed several hours behind schedule, turning what should have been an easy trip into a marathon.

Looking down a second later, Alicia was dismayed to find that her suitcases were gone. The man with the curt voice was walking off with them!

"Hey, you! Come back with those!" Alicia shouted.

The man kept right on moving, his cowboy boots eating up the distance between him and the nearest exit. Alicia finally caught up with him just as he was tossing the suitcases in the back of a dusty Bronco.

At close range, the man was definitely intimidating. His commanding height and rangy-yet-powerful build made her extremely glad that she'd stopped to get a policeman. This wasn't the kind of man you fought alone.

"There he is, Officer," Alicia stated. "And those are my two suitcases he's got."

Keeping one hand on the frame of the Bronco, the man turned his head to glance at her over his shoulder—wordlessly telling her she wasn't worth the effort of turning around completely. Alicia knew she was no beauty, but she couldn't believe this man's arrogant nonchalance as he cocked his Stetson back from his forehead, his gaze ambling past her to the policeman standing behind her.

"There some law against touching your suitcases?" he inquired.

Under the circumstances, Alicia thought his sardonic humor was inappropriate. Talk about a nervy thief! "You did more than just touch them. You walked off with them!"

"The lady said you were trying to steal her suitcases," the policeman inserted.

"Why would I want to do that?" the man retorted with a lazy drawl.

"I told you that those were my bags, but you took them anyway. Why?" Alicia demanded.

"Because that's what I was sent here to do," he replied.

"You'd better step away from the vehicle, sir," the policeman ordered.

For the first time, the man's unruffled attitude showed signs of impending frustration. Muttering a curse, he complied.

"Look, I just came here to pick her up," he said impatiently.

"I never met this man before in my life," Alicia stated with complete certainty.

"Do you know her, sir?" the policeman asked.

"We've never met," he admitted.

"See?" Alicia said triumphantly.

"But I do know her father," the man added.

"Then you should also know that my father is coming to pick me up," Alicia replied.

"That was the original plan, yes. But something came up at the lodge, and since I was already driving into Calgary to pick up some supplies, I said I'd pick you up."

Alicia eyed him suspiciously, clearly not believing a word he said.

"Do you have some identification, sir?" the policeman inquired.

Giving Alicia a black look that blamed her for this mess, the man reached into his back pocket and took out a thin, very worn wallet and flipped it open to what Alicia assumed was his driver's license. "Name's Mitch Johnson," he informed the police officer with a masculine geniality definitely at odds with the dark look he'd just given Alicia. "I work for her father." A jerk of his thumb indicated the "her" in this case.

Alicia tried to contain her simmering anger and instead focus her attention on recalling the name of the new handyman her father had hired last autumn. What had her father called him? John something-or-other? She couldn't remember for sure. But she certainly didn't appreciate Mitch Johnson's attitude, whether he worked for her father or not.

"You say my father was delayed at the lodge?" she asked the cocky cowboy with the attitude problem.

Mitch nodded, returning his wallet to his back pocket. "That's right."

"Then I should be able to call him and verify you're who you say you are," Alicia declared.

"Or you could just look at the side of the Bronco." He stepped away from the vehicle and indicated the lettering on the door that said Riverside Lodge—her father's lodge. "But go call, by all means, if it'll make you feel better." He gave the policeman a look that had *Women!* written all over it. "We'll just wait for you here." Having said that much, Mitch turned to the police officer and began discussing the Calgary Flames hockey team. Alicia had been dismissed.

She'd been coming to Calgary since she was seven years old, so she supposed she should have gotten used to the definitely masculine slant of the area by now.

She was twenty-nine. Calgary was cowboy country. Both statements were simple facts.

The man's claim to be picking her up was also factual, she discovered as she phoned her father.

"Sorry, pumpkin," her dad said. To her father, she'd never be twenty-nine, Alicia reflected affectionately. She'd always be "pumpkin," or in a crunch, "honey." "I was hoping to be there myself to pick you up, like I have every other year. But then Gloria got sick, and I didn't feel right leaving her." Gloria and Alicia's father had been married for twenty-two years now, and Alicia couldn't have hoped for a sweeter stepmother.

"Is Gloria all right?" she asked, immediately concerned.

"Yes. The doctor says it's nothing to be worried about. But since Mitch was already going into Calgary, I thought it would be okay for him to pick you up. What's wrong? Is there a problem?"

"No, Dad. No problem." At least not one that I can't handle, Alicia added to herself. "Just checking, that's all. Umm, this Mitch of yours. Is he about six feet tall? Has dark brown hair, blue eyes, a square chin and a lazy drawl?"

"You could have just described half the cowboys between here and Montana," her father replied.

"No, this one's different," she said slowly.

"Yep, that's Mitch," her father declared with satisfaction. "Different."

Alicia sighed. "Then I'd better go rescue him from the policeman's clutches."

"Policeman?" her father repeated in alarm.

"Nothing to worry about. When Mitch took off with my luggage, I thought he was trying to steal it.... Never mind, Dad. We'll work it all out. How's the weather up there in Jasper?"

"Clear as a bell. The mountains are really putting on a show for you. See you soon, pumpkin."

Alicia hurried back to the curb, torn between guilt at having falsely accused the man of stealing and impatience at his high-handed behavior, which in her opinion, had only exacerbated the situation.

It was immediately apparent to her that the two men had gotten along fine without her. In fact, they made her feel like an intruder as she joined them and consequently interrupted their hockey discussion.

Refusing to be intimidated, Alicia tried to make the best of a sticky situation. "Umm, I verified Mr. Johnson's story with my father. Apparently he was, indeed, sent here to pick me up, although why he didn't tell me so in the first place instead of taking off with my luggage, I don't know. Anyway, I'm sorry for the inconvenience, Officer."

"No problem, ma'am."

"What about me?" Mitch Johnson inquired after the policeman had gone. "Aren't you going to apologize to me, too?"

"What for?"

"For almost getting me arrested."

"I didn't almost get you arrested. *You* almost got *yourself* arrested. If you'd walked up to me and introduced yourself first, the way any reasonable person would have—"

"I never claimed to be reasonable," Mitch said with a shrug.

That wasn't very reassuring news for Alicia, since she was about to get into the Bronco with him. Being driven by an unreasonable man for four-hundred miles over mountain roads sounded a bit on the risky side to her. Maybe she should take a bus. She looked at her watch. It was a little after two. She'd missed the last bus for the day. Maybe the train . . .

"Well?" Mitch demanded impatiently as he held the door open for her. "Are you going to get in or not?"

"What? I don't get any time to think about it?" she retorted with mocking humor.

"Think about it? What's there to think about?"

"Do I really want to put my life in the hands of a man who is not only proud of the fact that he isn't reasonable, but also keeps a four-leaf clover in his wallet?"

She was surprised at the briefly disconcerted look that passed over his face. She only noticed it because she'd been studying him closely at the time. Her reasons for doing so were practical rather than sexual.

Now that she knew he *was* sent to pick her up, she looked at him carefully again, this time to determine if he was in any condition to drive. She felt sure her father only hired responsible people, but one could never be too careful.

He looked wide awake, even though his right eye sloped down a bit, contributing to his sleepy-eyed, devilish appearance. And the whites of his eyes were just that—white with no bloodshot little red lines. His hands were steady, even if he was clenching them at the moment. He looked capable of safely driving her to Jasper, and driving her nuts if she let him.

"You coming or not?" he practically growled.

"After such a generous invitation, how could I refuse?"

"Then get in."

Alicia got in, quickly moving her long legs out of the way, just in case he should be tempted to slam the door on her foot. He looked irritated enough to try it. He didn't slam the door, but he did close it enthusiastically.

A second later, Alicia heard heavy breathing in her ear and almost jumped out of her skin. Her muffled shriek was heard by Mitch, who immediately reopened her door.

"Now what's wrong?"

Out of the corner of her eye, Alicia saw the lolling tongue of a dog. An Irish setter, to be exact. "Your dog startled me, that's all. Nice doggy," Alicia murmured uncertainly. She didn't have much experience with large dogs, although she loved animals in general.

Mitch rolled his eyes. "Her name's Red, not doggy."

"Does she bite?"

"Only on command," he retorted with a dire look in her direction.

Alicia was not the least apprehensive. "How reassuring. Go bite him, Red," she suggested with teasing encouragement.

"Only on *my* command," Mitch added.

"Too bad."

"Bloodthirsty little devil, aren't you."

Alicia turned to look at him in surprise. No one had ever called her bloodthirsty, let alone a devil. *Softie, lifesaver, do-gooder*—these were all terms that had been applied to her with varying degrees of thankfulness or impatience. But never *devil*. "You think so?"

Mitch frowned, wondering why she looked so intrigued by his comment. "Look," he said uncomfortably, "maybe we got off on the wrong foot here. I didn't mean to be insulting...."

"I'm not insulted," she assured him.

He leaned closer to get a better look at her. "You're not?"

"No."

They looked into each other's eyes with the kind of curiosity normally reserved for space aliens and complicated crossword puzzles.

She had nice eyes, Mitch noted hazily, appreciating their expression more than their actual color. Her gaze was direct. Open. No pretenses. No lies. It had been a long time since a woman had looked at him like that—without expectations, with teasing acceptance.

"Well, that's okay then," he muttered, hurriedly stepping back to slam the door.

As he walked around the Bronco to get into the driver's side, Mitch took a moment out to talk to himself. Ray's daughter wasn't turning out to be anything like he thought she'd be. Ray had shown him her picture, had bragged about her being a librarian...or was it a schoolteacher? Anyway, Mitch had been expecting a mousy creature with a personality as plain as her looks. Instead, he'd found a woman with the guts of a goalie at a Stanley Cup play-off game.

If Alicia Donnelly had a mousy bone in her body, he'd seen no sign of it. She was fiery and feisty and not one to back down from a fight. But she was practical, too. After all, she had brought a policeman with her when she'd confronted him. That had taken some quick thinking on her part.

Granted, she looked better in person than she did in the photo, but still, she was no beauty. Not that Mitch was impressed by beauty these days. He'd been burned by a pretty face in the past, and he still carried the scars to prove it. These days he looked for more than physical beauty. Actually, these days he wasn't looking at all. He was minding his own business. "Or trying to, anyway," Mitch muttered to himself.

But this lady had caught him unprepared. She was like one of those deceptively mild-looking Mexican dishes that knock your socks off with the first bite. "Yeah, well just remember that you and Mexican food don't get along," he told himself.

Inside the Bronco, Alicia was fastening her seat belt and silently praising herself for even having gotten into the seat in the first place. Her entrance into her father's various vans, pick-up trucks and four-wheel-drive vehicles had always been "experiences to remember," as her father used to say. Wearing slacks helped. She'd learned that much, at least.

Alicia smiled as she tried to remember the last time she'd worn a dress for the trip here to Calgary. One moment in particular came to mind. She must have been about seven or so. Actually the dress hadn't gotten her in trouble that year, the shoes had. They'd been white and shiny, her best Easter shoes that she'd cried over until her mother had given in and let her wear them on the plane. Of course, they'd no sooner arrived in Jasper than she'd stepped into a mud hole up to her ankle. Her shoes had been ruined, just as her mother had predicted they would be. Alicia hadn't known what to do, but her dad had. He'd taken her into town and gotten her a lemon ice-cream soda and a pair of shiny white shoes to replace the ones she'd ruined. The memory was sweet. She couldn't wait to see her dad again.

As soon as Mitch got into the Bronco, he noticed that she was smiling. "What's so funny?" he demanded, trying not to sound too defensive. Had the woman somehow guessed he'd been out there talking to himself? He sure as hell hoped not.

Alicia blinked at him. "I beg your pardon?"

"It's a little late to be doing that," he retorted. "You should have begged my pardon after siccing that policeman on me."

"That's a matter of opinion."

"Yeah, well...you were smiling a minute ago. How come?"

"Does there have to be a reason?" she countered.

"Yes."

"Maybe I was just smiling to aggravate you," she suggested, her smile turning into a grin.

"Wouldn't surprise me. You've already shot the day's schedule to hell, what with your flight being so damn late and then that little fiasco with the law." He said it as if she'd arranged the entire thing on purpose just to frustrate him.

"While I'd like to accept the credit for single-handedly ruining your day, it simply wouldn't be fair for me to take it all myself. I have to share the honor with the airlines, without whose help I would never have managed to shoot your schedule to hell."

"I think you'd have managed it somehow," Mitch retorted dryly. "You seem like the type who can manage anything."

Alicia frowned. "What's that supposed to mean?"

"Don't get all riled up. It was a compliment."

"I'll bet," she muttered.

"You don't sound very convinced."

"I'm *not* convinced, but don't let it bother you."

But she did bother him, and Mitch couldn't for the life of him figure out why. He cast her a quick look as they stopped at a traffic signal outside the airport. She had a cute nose. Just a tad turned up at the end. The word *uppity* came to mind.

"Aren't you a teacher or a librarian or something like that?" he asked her.

"Something like that. And you're a handyman."

"Something like that."

"A challenging job, I'm sure."

"You got something against handymen?"

"No. Have you got something against elementary school librarians?" she shot back.

"No."

"Great. Then we should get along just fine for the next seven hours or so until we reach Jasper. Let me know if you'd like me to drive."

"Why would I want to do a dumb thing like that?" he countered.

"You might be tired."

"Honey, men like me don't get tired from a little drive in the country."

"It's more than a little drive." Another thought occurred to Alicia, momentarily preempting her protest over his use of the term *honey*. "You didn't drive in from Jasper *today* did you?"

"I got in last night."

"That's a relief."

"Not that I couldn't have made the round-trip in one day," he stated.

"Look, I'm sure you're a superman. But all I want is a good, sensible driver. Okay?"

"What makes you think I'm not a good driver?"

"I didn't say you weren't a good driver," she retorted in exasperation. It had already been a frustrating day for her, and he wasn't making things any easier. "It's just that I was in a bad car accident when I was in high school. The guy driving was my girlfriend's boyfriend, and he fell asleep at the wheel. We all survived, but I'd rather not repeat the experience, okay?"

"Okay." He immediately let up on the gas pedal. He wanted to tell her that, other than the one he'd gotten for parking at the curb at the airport today, he hadn't had a ticket in over five years. He wanted to reassure her that he'd take care of her, that she'd be safe with him. He couldn't think of any clever way of saying it, though, so he kept quiet. But he made sure that his driving was conservative, to say the least.

* * *

Alicia didn't relax until they'd left the city traffic of Calgary behind and were on the expressway leading to the mountains. Mitch hadn't said a word to her for the past half hour. At this rate, the trip to Jasper would be long, indeed. The silence was already driving her up the wall.

"So, tell me about yourself, Mr. Johnson," she suggested, determined to lighten the mood in the front of the Bronco.

"The name's Mitch."

She waited expectantly for more, but nothing else was forthcoming. Maybe he just needed more prompting. "And?"

"And what?"

"And what else were you going to say?"

"Nothing."

"You don't like talking about yourself," she noted quickly. "Okay, how about Red? Do you like talking about him?"

"Red is a bitch."

"That's no way to talk about your dog!"

"Bitch as in female dog."

"Right. I knew that." Alicia squirmed in her seat. She had a master's degree, for goodness sakes. She'd read the dictionary for fun as a kid. She knew all about words and their meanings. She *didn't* know about Mitch and at this rate, she wasn't sure she wanted to find out. She was beginning to think that this conversation idea wasn't such a brilliant one after all.

After a long silence, Mitch said, "I found her at the Humane Society."

"Who?"

"Red," he answered impatiently.

"Right."

"If you didn't want to know about my dog, you shouldn't have asked. I thought you were interested."

"I am interested. In Red, that is." This was going from bad to worse here, Alicia told herself. "She seems like a nice dog. Quiet, too."

Red picked that moment to put her head on Alicia's shoulder, as if in appreciation for the words of praise.

"At least your dog's friendly," Alicia muttered, not intending that Mitch should hear her.

But he did. "And I'm not friendly?"

"You said it."

"What gave you that impression?"

"Oh, I don't know." An element of sarcasm crept into her voice. "Must have been the way you walked off with my luggage without even bothering to introduce yourself to me. Or maybe it was that if-looks-could-kill glare you gave me at the airport. Then again, it could be the way you won't say more than ten words to me at a time. Take your pick."

"I've used more than ten words at a time," was all Mitch said.

Whereupon, Alicia said, "Oh, I give up!"

"Don't do that."

"Why not?"

"I'd hate to think that I'd won this battle so easily," he drawled.

"It's not a battle, and it's not a matter of winning."

"Isn't it?"

"No," she replied in exasperation. "It's called conversation, and it's what most people do to get to know each other, to be polite. But then, let me guess—you never claimed you were polite, right?"

He grinned. She watched the corners of his lips lifting, watched the crinkling lines appear in his suntanned cheek.

"You're getting to know me pretty well," he admitted. "Conversation or no conversation."

"Right. I know you guard your privacy, you like hockey and you have a dog named Red." She rubbed Red's ears and the dog closed her eyes in contentment. "Oh, and you also have a four-leaf clover in your wallet, but I suppose that's a forbidden subject, too."

Mitch shrugged. "It's just a memento from happier times."

"Are the times you're having now so unhappy?"

"I didn't say that. Why are women always twisting a man's words around?" he impatiently demanded of the world at large.

"Probably because men rarely say what they really mean," she replied just as impatiently.

"Why are you so curious, anyway?"

"I'm not curious. I was just trying to make conversation."

"Then maybe we should talk about you instead of me," he suggested.

"Then again, maybe we should talk about the scenery." They were nearing the entrance to Banff National Park, which would in turn, lead them to Jasper National Park. "It's beautiful, isn't it?" Alicia didn't even pause to wait for his answer because she figured that anyone in his right mind could see how spectacular the surrounding scenery was. Mountains, wild and rugged, reached for the sky, while brilliant meadows of green lay at their feet. "I miss it so much when I'm gone."

"Ever thought of moving up here?"

"All the time. But unfortunately my job is in Minneapolis. There aren't all that many openings for elementary school librarians here."

"There are elementary schools around here."

"A few, yes. Just not many openings in my field. But at least I get to spend my summers here, helping out my dad and Gloria at the lodge, pitching in wherever I'm needed. There's no place else I'd rather be.''

To his surprise, Mitch realized that there was no place else he'd rather be at that moment, either, than sitting right there in the Bronco next to Alicia, listening to her talk about the mountains she obviously loved. He liked the sound of her voice. It was rich and filled with warmth, with excitement, with life. And it carried a potent kick, like a shot of whiskey that slid down real smooth and only hit you later.

Mitch shook his head. He certainly had her tied up with food and drink in his mind. So long as she didn't become as necessary to him as either one of those two needs, he'd be okay.

As they drove on, Mitch was pleasantly surprised by her appreciation of the passing countryside. Nothing seemed to escape her notice. He found himself stealing more and more frequent looks at her just to catch a hint of the smile that lifted her lips whenever she saw something that pleased her, which was about every other mile.

''There's more snow on Castle Mountain than there was last year at this time,'' she noted after a period of silence.

''I wasn't here last year.''

''Where were you?''

''Around.''

''I've been there a time or two myself,'' she deftly replied, her grin downright mischievous. ''It's not as nice as it is here.''

To her surprise, he agreed with her. ''No, it's not as nice as it is here.''

''Can we stop for a minute at the next scenic pull off? I want to take a picture.'' She was already busy tugging her trusty 35-mm camera from her carry-on bag.

''We've got a long way to go yet. We can't be stopping at every scenic pull off, you know.'' But even as he was grumbling, Mitch had hit the turn signal, indicating he was turning off the highway. "Just one picture. And don't take all day."

"I think we could all use a stretch of our legs," Alicia returned. "Especially Red."

Looking over his shoulder, Mitch noticed the dog's agitation. "All right, all right." He got the leash out from the glove compartment and hooked it onto Red's collar. "Come on, girl. You at least do what you're told, don't you?" He noticed that Alicia was already on her third photo, this time of a playful prairie dog poking its head up from its burrow along the hillside. "Unlike some people, you know how to obey orders, don't you, Red?"

At which time, as if to deliberately disprove the comment, Red headed left when Mitch headed right. Since Red had more reason to head for the grassy verge on the left than Mitch did for heading right, he lost that particular battle. "Just don't go getting any ideas about declaring your independence," Mitch warned Red as they headed back to the Bronco. "I think she's a bad influence on you. Don't look at me with those big brown eyes of yours. You know what I'm talking about."

Red just tilted her head and gave him a doggy grin.

Alicia was waiting for him next to the Bronco. "Thanks for stopping. I got some really good shots." She smiled her appreciation.

"You really do love it here, don't you?"

"Absolutely. Who wouldn't?"

Mitch could think of at least one person who wouldn't— his ex-wife, Iris. She'd never cared about any beauty other than her own. And she'd certainly never have dirtied the knees of even her oldest slacks by crouching down to take a picture of a prairie dog the way Alicia just had. Not that Alicia's slacks appeared to be old by any means. They were actually quite nice, even with dirt stains on their knees.

"I mean, look how many people visit this area each year," Alicia said, bending over to brush off her slacks.

Mitch was too busy looking at her to answer.

"Millions of people come here from all over the world. In fact, together, the four parks—Banff, Jasper, Yoho and Kootenay National Parks—have all recently been declared World Heritage sites by the United Nations because of their outstanding beauty."

"And because they also include all four geological zones of the Rockies," Mitch said. Hey, he could read a map as well as the next guy, and the park map had listed that information. He'd read it when he'd first arrived at Jasper. The smile she gave him made him feel like he'd just scored a goal.

"That's right," she said. "You've done your homework."

"Spoken like a true elementary school librarian."

She grimaced. "Sorry about that."

"Don't be. It's nice to hear someone enthusiastic about something for a change."

"Sometimes I've got too much enthusiasm."

Mitch knew that most of the time, he didn't have any enthusiasm at all. He hadn't for a long time now. The realization made him feel uneasy. In fact, it made him downright uncomfortable.

"Let's get going," he said shortly. "We've wasted enough time here. You know, if you'd have flown into Edmonton instead of Calgary, it wouldn't take this long to get to Jasper."

"And I wouldn't get to see this view. Besides, I'm flying out of Edmonton. I do this each year, fly into one city and out of the other."

"Sounds like a waste of time to me."

Alicia frowned, wondering what had made him so crabby all of a sudden. She tried a few more times to start a conversation, but Mitch stubbornly remained quiet. So she just sat back and enjoyed the passing scenery and her favorite places en route—Waterfowl Lake and the Columbia Icefields.

They were close to Jasper when Alicia spotted an elk.

"Let's stop."

"What for?" Mitch questioned.

"For that elk."

"You've been coming up here for years. Don't tell me you've never taken a picture of an elk before."

"Well, I got a really good shot once of an entire herd on the golf course of the Banff Springs Hotel," she reminisced. "They were right around the nineteenth hole."

"Then you don't need to stop for this elk."

"Yes, I do. Please stop."

"We don't have time," Mitch stated brusquely. "We're already running late. There are plenty of other elk you can take."

She muttered something which sounded suspiciously like "Dictator!"

"Now what's the problem?" he demanded.

"I don't have a problem," she said stiffly. "Do you?"

"Sure. Lots of them. And I don't want to talk about any of them."

"Fine. Maybe we just shouldn't talk at all."

"Great idea."

But during those last silent thirty miles, Mitch found that he missed the sound of her voice. It was with much relief that he finally turned into the drive leading to the Riverside Lodge.

"This is it," Mitch announced. "The end of the line."

It may have been the end of the line, but Alicia had a feeling that her battles with Mitch Johnson were just beginning.

Two

Alicia heard the shouts of welcome before Mitch had even pulled the Bronco to a stop. Delighted, she turned to laugh and wave at the welcoming committee gathered on the porch of the sprawling stone lodge. After the strained silence of the past half hour, the warm reception made Alicia feel good. This was home. At least for the summer.

Before Mitch could even reach for his own door, Alicia had shoved hers open and gone racing up the stone steps to greet everyone.

Her dad met her with a bear hug that lifted her right off her feet. "Welcome home, pumpkin!"

Gloria was there, too. "It was only one of those darned migraines," she reassured a worried Alicia. "I'm feeling much better now. Your dad is just an old worrywart."

"Who are you calling old?" Ray protested, hooking an affectionate arm around Gloria.

As Alicia looked at the two of them, smiling at each other like a pair of teenagers instead of a married couple of over twenty years, she wondered with a slight pang if *she'd* ever experience the very special kind of love that they shared. There was little time for further reflection, however, as she was engulfed in yet another hug.

Out in the Bronco, Mitch's voice was curt as he ordered a boisterously barking Red to be quiet. The dog gave him a hurt look, as if asking why she couldn't participate in all the fun, too. Mitch looked away, his attention returning to the noisy goings-on up on the porch. In addition to Alicia's father and stepmom, there were two kids and a petite woman embracing Alicia. Alicia was in danger of being smeared with chocolate from the ice-cream cone the red-headed kid was eating, but Alicia didn't seem to notice, let alone care. Her face was lively with pleasure, her smile warm as she hugged and was hugged. Everyone was talking at once as they all turned and walked into the lodge.

With the closing of the lodge's massive front door, everything was suddenly quiet. Mitch was once again alone. Normally he liked the feeling. Right now he didn't.

"Come on, Red," he muttered. "Time for the hired help to unload the luggage." Mitch knew he had no cause to be grumbling, but his mood had been rotten since he'd spoken to his ex-wife earlier that morning. That's why he hadn't felt very social with Alicia, why he hadn't introduced himself before picking up her bags at the airport.

What he couldn't figure out was why he felt this strange sense of loss at Alicia's absence—as if the sun had disappeared behind a cloud. He absently rubbed Red's left ear as the dog followed him out of the Bronco. For a supposedly mild-mannered librarian, Alicia had certainly managed to throw him off balance.

While tugging the suitcases from the back, Mitch reflected on the return trip. It had gone by quickly, he had to admit that much. At least it had until the end there, when Alicia had clammed up.

Until then, he'd enjoyed hearing her talk about the summers she'd spent here as a child. Hell, he'd just enjoyed hearing her talk, period. She had a way about her. She made him feel like a man who, after stumbling around in the cold and the dark, had suddenly discovered the comforting light and beckoning warmth of a campfire.

Distracted as he was by his thoughts, Mitch wasn't expecting to bump into anyone when he turned around. Startled, he dropped one of the suitcases he was holding. It fell to the dusty ground with a thump, narrowly missing his foot.

Swearing softly but enthusiastically, he glared at Alicia—who stood there looking as if she were trying not to laugh.

"You know, Mitch, you've got a real way with words there," she noted with mocking admiration. "I don't think I've heard such a creative string of curses since my dad hammered his thumb last year. Just don't let the kids overhear you. Julie's got enough trouble keeping them under control."

"Is that what you came out here for?" he growled. "To lecture me?"

"Actually, I came out to see if you needed any help with the luggage. As you know, my dad's back is bad...."

"I don't need any help picking up two measly little suitcases," he curtly informed her.

"Your *attitude* could sure use some help!" she shot back.

"You don't like my attitude, you know what you can do."

"Yes, but I've sworn off kicking and punching unarmed men," she retorted sweetly. The look in her eyes was anything but. She held on to her temper by counting to five, in Latin. "Look, I don't want my dad knowing that we don't get along."

"I thought we got along just fine."

"Right," she scoffed. "When we don't speak to each other, we get along just fine. Since you don't need any help with the luggage, I'll go back inside."

She turned to leave, but his hand on her arm stopped her. It also stopped her heart. Anger, she told herself. It's the fight-or-flight adrenaline pumping through your system. That's all.

Wondering if he, too, felt the anger or whatever it was, she gazed into his blue eyes. There she saw a fleeting sense of surprise reflected by the momentary tightening of his fingers on her arm before he released her. "What room are you staying in?" he asked in a husky murmur.

"Why?" she returned suspiciously.

He smiled, and her heartbeat soared again. "I need to know where to put your suitcases."

"Upstairs, third door on the right." She belatedly remembered the girlish decor of the room, all pink stripes and white canopies. The room hadn't been redone since she was sixteen. She didn't want him seeing it, didn't want to give him any more ammunition with which to taunt her. "You can just leave the bags outside the door."

"Nonsense. I wouldn't want anyone tripping over them."

She should have figured he'd say that. Whatever she didn't want him to do, he did. Whatever she wanted him to do, he didn't want to do. Perverse. That's what he was. Good-looking, too—in a rugged Western sort of way. Not that his looks mattered to her one way or another. She knew better than to judge a book by its cover or a man by the sexual voltage of his smile.

"Lead the way," he invited as he easily hefted a suitcase in each hand.

She did. Reluctantly.

Upstairs, she made one last bid to stop him from entering her room. "That's fine," she said. "I'll take them from here."

"Forget it. Get the door for me."

As he strode by with her luggage, she couldn't resist sticking her tongue out at him.

"I saw that," he informed her as he dumped the bags at the foot of the bed. "Nice alligator." He lifted the stuffed toy off the bed. "You play with it often?"

She snatched it away from him. "It's not an alligator, it's a duck-billed platypus." She dropped the toy back onto the bed. "I've had this room since I was a kid," she said defensively. "It hasn't been changed much."

"You've changed, though," he noted, eyeing the picture of her that must have been taken when she was in grade school. She had braces on her teeth and was squinting at the camera. She looked skinny. She'd filled out nicely, he decided, stealing a quick look as she bent over the suitcase.

Alicia pulled out some of the goodies she'd brought for everyone and then turned to face Mitch. "Yes, well...thanks for carrying all this stuff upstairs for me." When he showed no sign of leaving, she added, "Everyone's waiting downstairs."

"Right." He slowly ambled over to the door. "Who's the lady with the kids?"

"Julie. She lives here in Jasper. She's a good friend of mine."

"Yeah, I got that impression from the way you two were hugging each other."

For just a fleeting second, there was a bleakness in his voice that Alicia responded to instinctively. "You're welcome to join us if you'd like." The words were out of her mouth before she could stop them, let alone think about them.

But Mitch once again had his male invincibility firmly in place. "Feeling sorry for me, are you?" he drawled. "Don't bother."

"Don't worry, I won't." She left him standing there on the stairs, convinced she must have imagined any momentary changes in his maddening attitude.

"You okay?" Julie asked Alicia downstairs after a curious look at Mitch's rapidly departing figure. "You seem a bit hot under the collar."

"It's that man." Alicia managed to fill the last word with every shred of her disgust.

But Julie just grinned. "Yeah, he is kind of good-looking, isn't he?"

"He's impossible, is what he is."

"Had an interesting drive from Calgary, did you?"

"Let's just say that we agreed to disagree."

"I sense sparks here, Alicia."

"Give me a break. The guy's not my type. Too rugged, too sure of himself, too moody."

Later that night, as Alicia tossed and turned in her narrow bed, she had second thoughts. Not about Mitch being her type, but about that moment on the stairs when she'd seen something in his eyes—something stark and hungry. She could have sworn that there had been a smoldering loneliness in those baby blues of his, and it had touched her.

"Maybe you're just plain touched!" she muttered, punching her pillow. The only reason a man such as Mitch was alone was because he *wanted* to be alone. Besides, her practical side pointed out, the guy had a very affectionate dog. It's not as if he was totally on his own.

Sighing, Alicia kicked off the covers and headed for the small window seat beneath her open bedroom window. The dotted Swiss curtains swirled in the cool breeze as she curled up on the faded pink pillows. The view from here had always soothed her restless thoughts in the past, maybe it would do the trick tonight, as well.

Outside her window, moonlight spilled down from a star-studded sky, bouncing off the shimmery water of the nearby Athabasca River. The rushing noise of the river was punctuated by the sound of a dog barking. Alicia wondered if it was Red.

She leaned a little closer to the window to get a better look. There was no sign of a dog, but there was a man riding out on a motorbike, the moonlight reflecting off his dark helmet. Alicia couldn't see him clearly, but she knew it was Mitch.

Once the solitary rider had disappeared from sight, Alicia returned to bed, feeling even more restless than she had before. When she finally did fall asleep, it was only to dream about a bike-riding cowboy who tossed her luggage around and gave her a bouquet of four-leaf clovers. It was no surprise that after a night spent that way, she'd wake up feeling confused.

When Alicia felt confused, she headed straight for the garden. There was nothing like a little solid dirt to put some perspective back into your day, she reminded herself resolutely. After stopping by the kitchen to steal one of the blueberry muffins Gloria had just baked, Alicia only stayed inside long enough to make sure her help wasn't needed anywhere else before heading outside.

The morning sunlight poured down through the surrounding Douglas fir and white spruce trees, creating a dappled quilt of light and shadow. The lighting was magical and had always reminded Alicia of an enchanted forest when she'd been a child. It could also have been Little Red Riding Hood's forest. In which case, Alicia knew all about the Big Bad Wolf—alias Mitch Johnson. For the time being, there was no sign of him. She told herself she was glad.

The reassuring familiarity of the lodge's rustic setting soon had Alicia feeling like her old self again. In a world where things seemed to move at the speed of light, it was comforting to find that everything here had stayed the same. The semicircle of cabins comfortably nestled in the woods still brought to mind campers gathered around a campfire—close enough not to get lonely, yet far enough away to retain their autonomy. The air smelled just the way she remembered—a unique mixture of woodsmoke from the cabin fireplaces, along with the invigorating scent of pine and the mouthwatering aroma of the freshly baked goodies that Gloria offered for sale to the guests each morning. Even the flowers waiting in the greenhouse for her to plant were exactly the same three varieties as in years past. Mums, marigolds and petunias. Lots of them.

An hour later, Alicia was humming to herself as she cheerfully dug another hole for the next petunia in the long line of them bordering the walk around the lodge. So involved was she with her gardening that the feel of something wet nudging her bare arm caught her completely by surprise.

Alicia's startled gasp was immediately followed by a muffled woof. "Red!"

An unrepentant Red frolicked away from Alicia's restraining hold. A second later, the dog was back, this time with a Frisbee in her mouth. She dropped it on top of the petunia Alicia had just planted.

"Don't play here!"

At the sound of her word *don't,* Red crouched down and looked so forlorn that Alicia was immediately overcome with guilt.

"Oh, all right." She picked up the Frisbee, noting that it had Mitch's name printed on it. "Here. Go get it!"

Wanting to get it as far from her flowers as possible, Alicia threw the plastic disk with all her might. It whirled rapidly through the air before hitting an unsuspecting Mitch as he rounded the corner of the lodge.

Alicia was at his side a moment later. "I'm so sorry! Are you all right?" She had to pose her question to his back because he was bent over.

Hearing her voice, he quickly straightened. Or tried to. "I'm fine."

"You don't sound very well." She eyed him with concern. "And you look rather pale, as well."

"Hell, so would you if you'd just been hit in the—" He clamped his mouth shut and settled for glaring at her.

"I'm sorry," she repeated. "I didn't see you coming." She hadn't seen where the Frisbee had hit him, either, but from the way he'd doubled over, it wasn't hard to guess. "Is there anything I can do?" she asked uncomfortably.

"I think you've done enough already, don't you?"

"I didn't hit you on purpose. Red wanted to play, so I—"

"Tried to emasculate her owner?"

"Of course not!"

"Then what were you doing?"

"Throwing a Frisbee. You got in the way."

"So now it's my fault, is it?"

"It was an accident. No one's fault. Although if you'd given me some warning of your approach before rounding that corner—I guess it doesn't matter," she said quickly, noting the way his face was darkening ominously. "Like I said, it was an accident. No one's fault."

"Yeah, well...I'll just stay out of *no one's* way for a while and see if that helps," he drawled sarcastically. "Come on, Red."

A second later, Alicia called after him. "Mr. Johnson."

He ignored her.

"Mitch!"

"What?"

"You forgot your Frisbee." She held it out to him.

His fingers brushed hers as he took the plastic disk from her. "You got any other weapons up your sleeve?"

"Nary a one." She held out her arms for his perusal. "See?"

Mitch saw all right. He saw her looking at him with laughter in her eyes. The warmth was back again. His satisfaction with that fact surprised him.

"You're safe from me," she teasingly assured him.

Mitch didn't know about that. Alicia certainly had a way of making him sit up and take notice, of capturing his attention and holding it. How *safe* could that be?

He mulled over that question as he repaired a leaky bathtub faucet in cabin fifteen. Too bad he couldn't come up with any answers. When he'd finished that job, a good two hours later, he was surprised to find that Alicia was still outside on her hands and knees, planting flowers. She'd made her way around to the opposite end of the lodge.

Her face was flushed. Sunburn, he predicted. The sleeveless T-shirt she wore left her arms exposed to the sunshine. The faded cutoffs revealed enough of her long legs to be tempting, although he doubted if she realized it.

"Still playing in the dirt?" he inquired.

She looked up in surprise. He'd crept up on her again. "Yes." She hastily shoved her hair out of her eyes. "How's your Frisbee injury doing?"

"I've recovered."

"Good. I'm glad to hear that."

"You're getting a sunburn," he told her. "Any idiot knows not to work out in the midday sun without a hat."

"You aren't insinuating that I'm an idiot, are you?" she countered with a narrow look.

Mitch wasn't sure how to answer that one, so he responded with a question of his own. "Where's your hat?"

"I don't wear hats," she informed him with all the haughty dignity of the queen of England.

Mitch ruined the effect by saying, "You've got dirt on your face."

"I know." Her look dared him to say or do anything about it. So she had dirt on her face. Too bad, she thought to herself crossly. What did he want from her? Perfection? "Don't let me keep you. I'm sure you've got more important things to do than complain about my appearance."

"I wasn't complaining."

"Then what were you doing?"

"Making an observation."

"Well, in the future, please keep your observations to yourself." The man had called her an idiot. She wasn't real pleased with him at the moment.

He didn't go away as she'd hoped he would. Instead he stood there looming over her. "Was there something else?" she asked with barely masked irritation.

"I'm no expert at gardening, but aren't the roots supposed to be in the ground and the flowers above ground?" he inquired, pointing at the petunia she'd just buried under a mound of dirt.

"You're just full of helpful hints today, aren't you?" she noted caustically.

"What are you so angry about? Talk about temperamental. Women!" he muttered with a long-suffering look heavenward. "Come on, Red." But instead of obeying him, the Irish setter bounded up to Alicia, knocking her onto her fanny and crushing several petunias in the process.

"Hey, are you okay?" Mitch asked as he tried to pull an exuberant Red away.

Alicia couldn't answer him, because she was being doggy licked all over her face.

"RED!" Mitch's bellow made the dog sit down and give him a woeful look. Mitch knelt beside Alicia, who was hiding her face behind her hands. Seeing the way her shoulders were shaking, he was struck with remorse. "Don't cry. It's okay. Where are you hurt? Do you think you broke anything?"

She shook her head, unable to speak.

"I'm sorry," he repeated.

A moment later, the mirth Alicia had been trying to restrain erupted as she laughed herself silly.

"What's so funny?" he demanded indignantly.

"Everything. I've been touched by doggy lips! As Lucy would say—yuck!"

Mitch was lost. "Who's Lucy?"

"From the Peanuts comic strip. You know. Charlie Brown and friends?" Seeing the concern in his blue eyes, she said, "I'm sorry." She put her hand on his shoulder. "I didn't mean to scare you." Feeling the warmth of his skin beneath the thin cotton of his work shirt, she quickly removed her hand from temptation.

To her chagrin, she'd left a muddy handprint behind. "I didn't mean to ruin your shirt, either," she added dolefully. "This doesn't seem to be my day."

He captured the hand that was trying to pluck pieces of mud from his shirtfront. "Still mad at me?" he asked softly.

The look in his eyes confused her. It was intimate and sensual. Darkly inviting. Heated. Men didn't look at her that way. Especially not when she was sitting in the middle of a petunia patch with mud on her face, not to mention other portions of her anatomy.

"Mad at you? I haven't decided yet." She was also perplexed by the way he made her feel so shockingly and sensually alive! "Let me think about it."

"You do that."

Suddenly aware that she was sitting there staring at him like a star-struck adolescent, she struggled to find something else to say. "Sorry about messing up your shirt."

Mitch shrugged. "It'll wash out."

"I'm not usually this clumsy."

"Red would make anyone clumsy. Here, let me give you a hand up."

When he took hold of her hand, there was no lightning bolt of electricity as she'd expected. Instead, she felt a slow, compelling warmth that traveled all the way down to her toes, making them curl in her sandals. He was incredibly strong. He tugged her to her feet with enough force to almost knock her over again.

Mitch quickly steadied her by putting his hands on her shoulders. "Gee, you're a real flyweight," he noted in surprise.

"Yeah, I just look tough."

He removed his hands, but kept his eyes on her. "You don't look tough to me."

"No?" His visual caress left her breathless. Luckily it didn't leave her mindless or speechless, as well, for which she was grateful. "Right now, I just look muddy."

"You're not the only one," he noted with a rueful look at his own mud-spattered jeans.

She was relieved that he hadn't tried to claim that she looked wonderful. She wouldn't have believed him if he had said it. She knew it wasn't true. On her best days, she might rate five out of ten, but today did not qualify as even one of her better days. "Well, gee," she drawled, "it's been fun playing in the mud with you and Red, but I've got to go now. Just stay away from the petunias, okay? You step on 'em and you gotta replant 'em."

"Hear that Red?" Mitch said.

The dog woofed.

Mitch tipped his Stetson. "We'll behave, ma'am."

So will I, Alicia vowed. Hear that, heart? Behave. Settle down. Or else.

* * * *

"So, Mitch, what do you think of my daughter?" Ray Donnelly asked later that afternoon. He carefully kept his distance from where Mitch was chopping firewood with a vengeance.

Mitch paused long enough to wipe the sweat from his brow. "You didn't tell me she was such a firebrand."

"Alicia?" Ray said in amazement. "We are talking about my daughter, right? Quiet, sweet?"

"Hell on wheels," Mitch stated succinctly.

"No one's described her that way since she was four years old. Then she was into everything. But she's not like that anymore."

"No?"

"No."

Mitch tossed a splintered log out of the way before turning to face Ray. "Hey, I didn't mean it in a negative way."

"I know you didn't. It's just that I can't imagine my little pumpkin as a firebrand."

"Your little pumpkin has grown up," Mitch noted dryly.

"So she keeps telling me."

"And she throws a mean Frisbee."

"Really? I've never known her to be athletic. She usually prefers books to games."

"Oh, I imagine she's pretty good at playing games." Feminine games. The kind women seemed to be so good at. Look what she'd done to him today, tied him in knots.

"Alicia's usually good at anything she puts her mind to," Ray said with paternal pride.

Somehow that announcement didn't make Mitch feel any better.

Mitch didn't see Alicia again until just before sunset. Now that it was June, twilight lasted longer and occurred a little later every day. Mitch stood next to his motorbike and enjoyed the mellow light. This was his favorite time of day, when his work was done and he could hit the open road, leaving his problems behind.

Hearing the lodge's screen door slam shut, he looked up to see Alicia standing on the porch. She'd cleaned up nicely, he noted with a grin. The sundress she wore was demure yet flirty. Just like her.

Watching him put on the black helmet, she said, "Darth Vadar, I presume?"

"Does that mean I'm supposed to sweep innocent princesses like you off their feet?" he returned after removing the headgear to get a better look at her.

"You must have me mixed up with someone else," she replied. "I'm no princess."

"Royalty is in the eye of the beholder."

She briefly wondered if he was making fun of her. "Maybe you should have your vision checked."

"My vision or my head," Mitch muttered to himself. What he was about to do didn't make any sense, yet he knew he was going to do it anyway. "Want to come with me?"

"Come with you where?"

"On the bike."

Alicia was tempted to accept. Just to prove something. But then common sense reasserted itself and she shook her head. "No, thanks."

"Scared?" he taunted her.

"Just cautious."

"You always think before acting?"

"Usually."

"Too bad."

"Don't you?" she asked.

"Don't I what?"

"Think before acting?"

"Apparently not," he muttered under his breath. Why had he invited her to join him? He'd never felt the need for company before. Why now? And why her?

With regret and a strange longing, Alicia watched him roar off into the distance. Leaning against the porch railing, she reminded herself that she'd done the right thing in refusing his invitation. She wasn't dressed for a bike ride, for one thing. For another, he was probably just being polite when he'd asked her.

Since when has Mitch been polite?

Okay, then maybe he'd only been teasing her. Inviting her because he knew she'd refuse. That just made her wish she'd accepted him, after all.

She sighed. Mitch certainly had a way of provoking militancy in her. She wasn't usually this contrary. But he seemed to bring out a side of her she wasn't even aware still existed. A rebellious side, a wilder side.

Looking out over the once-soothing scenery, Alicia had a feeling she was going to have a hard time sleeping again tonight.

She was right.

Two days later, Alicia met Julie for lunch at one of the newer restaurants in town. "So fill me in on everything that's happened," Julie said to Alicia as soon as the waiter left. "We didn't really get a chance to talk when you got in the other night. We've got a lot to catch up on. You can start by telling me what's going on with you and the handyman."

"Nothing's going on. Here, try some of this ranch dressing on that salad of yours." Alicia shoved the crockery pot across the table toward her friend.

"No, thanks." Julie speared a cherry tomato with her fork and then reprimandingly aimed it at Alicia. "And quit trying to change the subject."

"Don't talk with your mouth full," Alicia retorted with a grin.

"Easy for you to say," Julie grumbled. "You're not on a diet. I didn't order this salad by choice, you know. I ordered it out of necessity."

"Same here," Alicia replied.

"You? On a diet?" Julie shook her head in disbelief. "No way. When we were growing up, you could eat anything and never gain a pound. I always hated you for that," she noted cheerfully.

"And I always hated you for having such wonderful curly hair when mine is as straight as a board," Alicia returned. "But then, if you can't hate your friends, who can you hate, right?"

"Right." Julie grinned. "How long *have* we known each other now?"

"Don't ask."

"No, really. Isn't this our twentieth anniversary or something?"

Alicia nodded.

"That means you must be . . ."

"Twenty-nine," Alicia said. "Don't rub it in."

Julie looked surprised. "Is your age starting to bother you? It never did before."

"I've never been almost thirty before. I mean, look at you. You're only two years older than me, and you've already got two kids."

"And the stretch marks to prove it."

"You know what I mean. Sometimes it feels like life is passing me by."

"You want kids? Feel free to borrow mine anytime."

"I've already had offers to borrow someone else's kids, thanks," Alicia noted cynically.

"You're talking about that twerp you were almost engaged to last year, aren't you. The one with the three monsters he attempted to pass off as boys?"

"That's the one." He was also the one who'd only asked her to marry him to provide a mother figure for his hell-raising kids. Their own mother had left to "find herself" and wanted no part in further child rearing.

Unfortunately, Alicia had only discovered those details after she'd gotten emotionally involved with Rob. She'd been foolish, and it still hurt. She'd never forget the burning humiliation she'd felt when she'd overheard Rob talking to one of his co-workers at his company's Christmas party. In a voice slurred by alcohol, Rob had referred to her as "a cold fish with plain looks." The rest of his comment was forever etched in Alicia's mind—"At least I'll know where she is at night, know what I mean?" Rob had laughed slyly. "She'll be home taking care of my kids. Why else do you think I'm going with her?"

The sound of Julie's voice jogged Alicia's mind back to the present.

"He was cow dung!" Julie declared.

"Yes, he was," Alicia agreed. "But how do you know that? You never met him."

"I didn't have to meet him. Anyone who doesn't appreciate you has to be cow dung. Or worse. The twerp took advantage of your generous nature."

He'd done more than that, Alicia noted. He'd just about destroyed her self-esteem, not to mention making her seriously doubt her own judgment. Alicia had never had any false illusions about herself. In school, her looks had been referred to as "mousy." One summer, at the tender age of fifteen, she'd dyed her hair blond in a fit of rebellion.

It hadn't helped. She'd had an allergic reaction to the peroxide, and her hair took weeks to recover. She'd looked ridiculous. Luckily the strange off-white color had disappeared by the time she'd returned to school, vowing never again to tamper with the light brown hair, brown eyes and average build that nature had bestowed upon her.

The bottom line was that it had taken Alicia a long time to accept who she was, to be comfortable with herself, and she refused to let Rob ruin all that. It was hard, though.

"You're too nice to people, too trusting," Julie was saying. "You're just a softy. Always have been."

"Not anymore." Alicia squared her shoulders. "I'm going to get tough."

Julie didn't look very convinced. "Sure you are."

"I mean it. I'm tired of being taken advantage of. Now that I think about it, do you know how many times I've loaned out money and never gotten repaid?"

"Is this your way of telling me you're not going to pay for lunch?" Julie inquired with a grin.

Alicia looked horrified. "Of course not."

"I didn't think so. What happened to getting tough?"

"Well, not with you."

"Mmm-hmm. And not with the waitress, either," Julie noted, eyeing the sizeable tip Alicia left.

"You heard what she said. She's working her way through college," Alicia said defensively.

"Right. You're still a pushover."

"I wouldn't say that. I successfully avoided your questions about Mitch Johnson, didn't I?" Alicia countered archly.

"Only temporarily. I'm not letting you off the hook that easily. Next time we talk, I'll want a full report."

"On what?"

"On whatever."

"I'm not in the market for 'whatever,'" Alicia informed her in exasperation. "Why is it that all my married friends keep trying to play matchmaker? They see a budding romance around every corner."

"It's easy. We want you to be as miserable as we are."

"Right. You really look miserable," Alicia noted wryly. "That grin on your face tells me exactly how bad off you are. And heaven knows that living with a charming man like David would drive anyone into the depths of despair."

"My husband is charming, isn't he?" Julie agreed with satisfaction. "But he's also been watching the kids for the past few hours. I'd better get back before they blow up the house. And you're not off the hook about Mitch Johnson yet. See you."

The next time Alicia saw Mitch he was sitting astride his motorbike, again at twilight. She told herself she'd come outside to enjoy the sunset, not to enjoy him.

"Change your mind?" he asked her.

"About what?"

"Coming with me on my bike."

She paused a moment and then said, "No."

"Still thinking too much." He shook his head disapprovingly. "Too bad."

The next evening, Mitch's invitation consisted of a raised eyebrow and a you-don't-know-what-you're-missing look in her direction. The invitation may have been unspoken, but it was there all the same. She was standing a mere foot away from him. She couldn't miss it. Nor was there any misreading of his confident assumption that she was too timid to take him up on his visual offer.

"Ready to go for a spin yet, princess?" he drawled.

This time Alicia didn't hesitate for one second. "Sure! What are we waiting for?"

Three

"Are you serious?" Mitch asked with obvious skepticism.

"Don't I look serious?" she returned irritably. She had enough second thoughts of her own, she didn't need him adding his two-cents worth. "How do you get on this thing?"

"Carefully." He took her hand, preventing her from trying to hop onto the back of the bike. "There's something you have to do first."

"Sign up for life insurance?" she suggested with humor meant to hide her nervousness.

"No. Biking is safe if you know what you're doing. And I do. Besides, studies show that more people are hurt going fishing than biking."

"Really? What study was that?"

"My own study. The one time I went fishing, I fell out of the damn boat and almost drowned. I've never had so much as a scratch from biking."

"Knock on wood when you say that," she warned him, reaching over to rap on a nearby cedar planter.

"Superstitious, are you?"

"What kind of question is that coming from a man with a four-leaf clover in his wallet?" she retorted. "So what is it I have to do before riding the bike?"

He opened a storage compartment at the back of the bike before answering her. "You have to put both these on." He'd pulled out a black leather jacket and a helmet similar to his own, only slightly smaller.

He held the jacket out for her first. She eyed him...and then the jacket, which looked as if it had recently come off the back of some hard-core biker. He had to be kidding, she decided, although she saw no sign of it in his expression.

"What's the problem?" he demanded impatiently.

With a philosophical shrug of her shoulders, Alicia reminded herself that she'd never worn black leather before. Maybe it would make a fashion statement. When she slid her arms into the sleeves, they reached halfway down her hands. Her shoulder-length hair was trapped beneath the coat's collar, but before she could reach up to free it, Mitch had done it for her—with surprising gentleness.

"There." He nodded his approval. "Put this on and you'll be all set."

She managed to put on the helmet he handed her, but had trouble with the strap.

"I'll do it," he said, moving her fingers aside. His fingers brushed her chin, warming her skin with his touch.

"Okay?" he asked softly.

Not trusting her voice, she nodded.

Putting on his own helmet, he got on the bike first, steadying it with splayed legs, feet firmly planted on the ground.

"You're next," he told her. "Get on and put your arms around my waist."

She did, sitting so close to him that she might as well have been glued to him.

Turning his head so that she could hear him, he spoke above the throaty engine noise. "Ready?"

Alicia leaned forward, resting her chin on his shoulder as she made her reply. "Ready."

When they headed out, Alicia realized she didn't have a clue where they were going, and she didn't care. Maybe it was the black leather, maybe it was Mitch, but she was feeling decidedly reckless at the moment.

That recklessness wavered slightly once they pulled onto the main highway and she saw how fast the pavement was whizzing by. Although tempted, she stoically refused to close her eyes. Actually, she figured that not seeing where they were going would only make her feel worse. Besides, now that she was getting a little more used to it, she decided that this motorbike riding might not be so bad after all. It got even better once Mitch slowed down to pull onto a small road leading out of Jasper. She knew the route well. It led to Pyramid Lake, one of her favorites.

Freedom. The ride symbolized it, and Alicia enjoyed it far more than she thought she would. Still, she held on tightly to the rocklike stability of Mitch. He made her feel safe, even if it was a safety laced with excitement.

They stopped at the first lake they came to. Although it was after nine-thirty at night, the sun was just beginning its leisurely chromatic display—otherwise known as sunset.

Alicia got off the bike first, rather pleased with the way she'd accomplished the tricky maneuver. She—who had trouble getting into a van without help. It had to be the leather jacket. She'd dismounted like a pro!

Noticing her self-congratulatory grin, Mitch smiled as well. "Proud of yourself, are you?"

"Somebody has to be," she returned without the slightest hesitation.

Mitch wanted to tell her that *he* was proud of her but once again, words failed him. You've really been in the mountains too long, he told himself in disgust. You've lost your touch.

He'd never been the tongue-tied type before. He'd always known the right thing to say to women. He'd been out in the cold so long, he wondered if he knew how to deal with the promising warmth Alicia offered. One thing he was sure of, though, and that was that he wanted to get close to her to see if this tug of attraction was real, to see if *she* was real.

He moved to her side, ready to slip his arms around her, when the wail of a child split the air. He and Alicia turned at the same moment. The sound had come from a car parked alongside the lake. The car appeared to be deserted except for the screaming child. Alicia rushed over.

"There, there," she soothed through the partially opened window. "It'll be all right."

The child, a little boy of about three, continued screaming for his mother. "She'll be right back," Alicia reassured him. Indeed, out of the corner of her eye she could see a young couple hurrying to the car. "Look over there, is that your mommy?"

The little boy nodded and hiccuped. His crying stopped as Alicia reassuringly held the chubby little hand he'd thrust through the window opening. "See, she's coming. She'll be right here. It's okay now." Her voice had automatically slipped into the soothing tone she used with frightened kindergartners.

"What are you doing to my baby?" the woman demanded with offended outrage.

"I'm trying to comfort him. What were you doing leaving him alone in the car that way?"

"We were only gone a few minutes. We stopped to take some pictures and didn't want to wake him. Stop crying, Billy," she ordered the child, giving him a slight shove through the open window. "You're giving mommy a head-ache!"

The couple then got in the car and drove off without so much as a thank you to Alicia for her attempts to help their child.

"You're good with kids," Mitch noted from her side.

"Yeah, it's their parents who drive me nuts sometimes," she muttered. "The most important job in the world—parenting—yet they let any dunderhead do it. No training required. No brains required. No compassion."

"You appear to have plenty of that. You'd make a good parent."

She knew he meant the words to be complimentary, but they hit a sore point with her. Bob had once said the same thing to her. "It's an occupational hazard," she said irritably. "Working with kids the way I do, everyone thinks I should take over their job as parents or become their unpaid baby-sitter. It drives me crazy!" Noting Mitch's disconcerted expression, she said, "Sorry. I didn't mean to dump on you like that."

"No problem."

Alicia turned back to the scenery, using it to calm herself. The lake's emerald-and-sapphire water mirrored the spruces bordering the shore, creating a picture-perfect upside-down image. Alicia was feeling rather upside-down herself at the moment. Taking a deep breath, she wiped memories of Rob from her mind and replaced them with the serene images of beauty all around her. She wondered if Mitch had somehow known that this was one of her favorite stops. "What made you choose this particular place tonight?" she asked him.

Mitch shrugged. "There's a photograph on the wall of one of the cabins that I like a lot. It looks just like this view."

His reply pleased her. "It *is* this view. I know. I took it."

"You did?"

"Yes. Why the surprised look?"

"It's good."

"Thank you."

"No, I mean it's *really* good. Professional quality. You must have a lot of experience."

If you only knew, Alicia thought to herself with a grin, instantly thinking of experience other than photographic. Taking a closer look, she noticed the upward slant of his nicely shaped upper lip. Was he thinking along the same lines? Could he be laughing at her—couching a very personal question in impersonal terms?

Actually, there was little about Mitch that she found to be impersonal. She already knew he had a way of saying one thing while meaning another. Yet he could be disarmingly direct when he chose to be.

"Experience?" she repeated with a *Mona Lisa* smile of her own. "I suppose I do have some. But mostly I just dabble."

"Dabble?" he croaked through a throat that had suddenly gone dry. Had she deliberately wet her lips just for his benefit? He already knew how delectable her mouth looked. She didn't have to draw his attention to the fact. He already wondered if those passionately curved lips of hers would taste as luscious as they looked.

"Yes, dabble. I take as many photographs as I can. As many as cranky drivers allow me to take," she amended teasingly.

"Still upset that I wouldn't stop so you could take that elk on the drive from Calgary?"

"It's hard to get good shots from a moving vehicle, but that's not the only reason I was upset. I don't like having my freedom restricted that way—being told by someone what I can or can't do."

"We all have restrictions, one way or another."

"You don't seem to," she noted.

"Yeah, well, appearances can be deceiving."

"You mean you're not the footloose, fancy-free loner you appear to be?"

"No one's completely footloose, as you put it. We've all got certain responsibilities."

"And what are your responsibilities?"

"Feeding Red twice a day. Keeping the cabins all in working order. Fitting in a sunset every once in a while."

"Is that all you want out of life?" she asked.

"What else is there?"

"A family. A home."

He shifted uncomfortably. "How did this conversation get so serious anyway?"

"I've no idea," she innocently returned.

"Getting back to what we were talking about before..."

"My...dabbling?"

"Right. You should do more than just...dabble."

"I should, should I?"

He nodded. "Seems a shame to waste talent like that."

She knew they were talking about an entirely different talent than photography. "You think so?"

"Definitely. A God-given talent like that should be used...frequently...for someone who'd appreciate it."

"Too bad I don't know anyone who'd appreciate it."

"You know me."

"Not really. Not yet. But I'm working on it." She'd had no idea that teasing him could be this exhilarating. It was rather like tweaking the tail of a temporarily good-natured tiger. She just hoped she didn't end up as tiger bait.

Mitch tossed an impatient look at an approaching group of teenagers, then bestowed a clearly challenging smile upon Alicia. "Maybe we should continue this discussion some-place a little less crowded."

"Maybe we should." She tried to keep her amusement from her voice. She recognized a dare when she heard one. "Pyramid Lake is right down the road. If you like the view from here, you'll like the view from there even more."

"Who's talking about the view?"

"We are."

"Not me."

"So you don't want to see one of my favorite places?" she returned, trying to look offended.

There was plenty he wanted to see—her without the oversize leather jacket, her without the rest of her clothes.... The realization caught him by surprise. Alicia wasn't what he'd call his type—blond and busty. A few years ago he might not have even given her a second look. But now . . . now he wanted a third and a fourth look. And each time, he saw something new in her, discovered yet another facet. She flirted like a pro, yet there was a delicious shyness mixed with the exultation in her eyes—she'd looked the same way when getting off his bike, as if surprised she'd done it so well.

He'd had a feeling from the very beginning that Alicia was special. One of a kind. He still wanted to kiss her. Another round of teenager laughter reminded him that this wasn't the place. Maybe Pyramid Lake would be....

Twilight was so prolonged at this time of year that the sunset hadn't diminished much once they reached their next destination a few minutes later.

"Hey! Where are you going?" Mitch demanded as Alicia expertly hopped off the bike and headed for a dirt path that dead-ended in a bunch of bushes. On second thought, he realized that may not have been a very judicious question, considering the fact that they were several miles from the nearest bathroom facilities.

But Alicia merely laughed over her leather-clad shoulder and held up a beckoning finger. "Follow me."

He did, and when he caught up with her, she was leaning over the railing on a wooden bridge that went from the lake's shoreline over to a tiny island. The path that had looked like it went nowhere had instead led him to an unexpectedly beautiful view. Somehow he found that fitting, considering that Alicia had been the guide. She, like the path, was more than she at first glance appeared to be.

"Look," she said excitedly, "the water's so clear you can see the little fish down there. There are hundreds of them."

Mitch obligingly looked, observing once again how much she noticed little things. And she didn't just notice them, she took simple pleasure in them. It was a trait he'd found rare in women—or in men for that matter.

Apathy was obviously not in Alicia's vocabulary. It *had* been in his for far too long. He wanted to change that. Sharing her excitement was the first step.

Alicia's attention quickly moved from the gliding fish to the glowing sky. She'd seen more mountain sunsets than she could count, yet they still moved her with their beauty for—like snowflakes—no two were alike. At the moment, the lower portions of the mountains were deeply shaded while the loftiest snow-covered peaks were fully exposed to the sinking sun's crimson light. To Alicia's eyes, they seemed like pyramids of fire.

Mitch didn't know which he enjoyed more—the showy sunset or the admiration on Alicia's face as she watched it. It didn't take him too long to decide that watching Alicia beat even the best that Mother Nature had to offer. Her face was so alive; her brown eyes sparkling with excitement and pleasure, her tempting lips lifted in an appreciative smile. The only time he'd seen his ex-wife looking one-tenth as excited had been when she'd dragged him along to go fur-coat shopping.

A sudden breeze blew a strand of Alicia's baby-fine hair over her lips. Mitch lifted his hand to brush it away but she beat him to it. He sighed regretfully.

"Something wrong?" she asked.

He shook his head while absently rubbing his hip. The old injury was acting up. Standing in one place for too long without moving did that to him sometimes. "Maybe we should find a more comfortable seat for this show," he suggested.

By mutual agreement, they headed for the island where they sat down on a handy boulder along the shoreline. They stayed to enjoy the final moments of the rosy splashes of light illuminating the pristine snow-capped peaks.

Sitting there, with Alicia close by his side, Mitch experienced a sense of peace he hadn't felt in years. "This is the life," he declared with quiet satisfaction.

Alicia murmured her agreement and nuzzled her chin into the soft leather. Now that the sun was all but gone, its heat had disappeared with it and the air was getting a little chilly.

Her movement caught Mitch's attention. "Maybe we should get back. Your parents will be wondering what happened to you."

"They saw me ride off with you."

"That's what I mean."

"My dad won't worry."

"You're his little pumpkin. He'll worry," Mitch stated dryly.

"My dad trusts you."

"Maybe he shouldn't," he said, considering all the lascivious thoughts he'd had, and was still having, about her. "We're out here in the middle of no place. Anything could happen."

"Is this the point where you tell me you're a wanted criminal on the run?" she asked with an ingenuous smile.

"We're all on the run in one way or another."

"And in which way are you on the run?"

"In all the ways a normal thirty-two-year old man is on the run."

"Ah." She nodded sagely. "You mean you're on the run from commitments."

He neither denied nor confirmed it. He merely said, "It's better than being on the run from the law."

"Can't argue with you there."

"It must be the first time you haven't argued with me."

"You do seem to bring out my defiant side," she acknowledged.

"Yeah, I noticed that. Your dad seemed pretty surprised when I told him you were hell on wheels. He seemed to think you were this sweet and quiet librarian."

"I am a sweet and quiet librarian. Sometimes. Other times I'm—"

"Hell on wheels," he supplied with a slow smile.

"Not many people see me that way."

"Their loss."

"In fact, most people I know would be surprised that I even got on that motorbike with you. *You* were surprised."

"I knew you'd say yes eventually," he claimed.

"Oh?" She snuggled deeper into the leather coat before turning to look at him. "And how did you know that? Did you think your charm would be too strong for me to resist?"

"So you think I have charm, eh? That's encouraging." He slipped an arm around her shoulder, tugging her a little closer to his own body warmth. "No, I knew you wouldn't be able to resist your own curiosity or that devil on your shoulder egging you on."

Having his arm around her felt so right, as if something missing had just been found. "*You* were the one egging me on. Accusing me of being scared, of being too cautious."

"It worked, didn't it?"

"Didn't your mother ever teach you it's impolite to gloat?"

"My mom died when I was nine," he said matter-of-factly. "I was raised by my dad. He taught me to play fair and not to spit in public. He never said anything about gloating."

"It sounds like the two of you get along pretty well."

She could feel his shrug. "We do okay. He's a pretty good guy. Your dad reminds me of him, except my dad hates snow. That's why he's moved to Arizona. He's retired now."

"Do you have any brothers or sisters?" Alicia asked.

"One older brother."

"Me, too. We came up to Jasper together when we were kids. My brother's got a family of his own now. They don't get up here very often anymore. But then, my brother never seemed to enjoy it here in the mountains as much as I did."

"And still do."

"And still do," she agreed.

"Ever been here in the winter?"

She nodded. "A few times. I'd love to see it in the fall, though. It must be spectacular with all the brilliant colors of the changing trees."

"Yeah, fall's not bad."

"Your enthusiasm overwhelms me," she teased him.

"I haven't had much to be enthusiastic about lately," he admitted slowly. "But I have a feeling that's about to change."

"I'm glad to hear it."

Mitch was glad, too—glad she'd agreed to come with him tonight. She was as refreshing as the pine-scented air. And she looked so adorably out-of-place in that tough black leather jacket that he felt surprisingly protective of her. She stirred those feelings in him, but she was hardly a clinging vine that needed constant care. She could look out for herself. He wanted to preserve that fire she had, wanted to protect the warmth of her. He didn't want to see that passion snuffed out. God knew there were few enough inner fires burning in anyone these days. Instead, so many people seemed driven by cool greed or bogged down by bored indifference.

"So, were you impressed by this evening's performance?" Alicia inquired.

"Floored." He stared down at her upturned face.

"I was talking about the sunset."

"Right. The sunset. They last longer here than they do in Colorado," Mitch noted absently, distracted as he was by the upward curve of her smile.

"Is that where you're from? Colorado?"

He nodded. "I grew up there. Outside of Denver. A sleepy little town called Idaho Springs."

"How did you end up here in Canada?"

He gazed off into the distance as if mentally reviewing the steps that had brought him there. "My dad's from Edmonton, originally. It's one of the reasons he hates snow. He met my mom while she was up here on a skiing trip. After they were married, he moved down to Colorado with her."

"There's a lot of snow in Colorado, too," Alicia pointed out, delighted that he was telling her so much about himself.

"I know. But that's where she was from, and she missed her family."

"If you grew up in Colorado, then the Rockies are nothing new to you."

"They look different up here, though. Sharper. Greener."

"That's because here in Canada there's no logging allowed in the national park. When you come up here, you realize what a real forest looks like."

"It looks even better from the back of a horse."

"You ride?"

He looked both insulted and shocked by the question. "Of course, I ride! Doesn't everyone?"

"I don't. I fell off a horse when I was eleven and broke my ankle. I decided horses and I weren't meant to be."

"Haven't you heard that when you fall off a horse, you've got to get right back on again?"

"I did, and the next time I broke my arm!"

"Maybe you're just accident-prone."

"Haven't you ever broken any bones?"

"Plenty of times." His face tightened as he rubbed his hip with his free hand.

"Are *you* accident-prone?"

"Some might say I am," he replied in a grim voice.

Even in the dim light, she could see the harsh lines of his face, the pain in his eyes. "I'm sorry," she said softly. "Am I bringing up unhappy times?"

"Yeah." He drew in a deep breath, refusing to let the dark thoughts overwhelm him. He'd come so far. He'd begun sleeping nights again—instead of staring into the darkness, refusing to close his eyes to avoid the tormenting images that had haunted him for so long. He wouldn't allow himself to be dragged into that abyss again. "Yeah, you are."

"Then we'll change the subject." She turned her face skyward again. "Which one is the Big Dipper?" she asked, pointing up to the approaching night sky.

"You're a schoolteacher and you don't know which one is the Big Dipper?"

"I'm a librarian, not a teacher."

"Even worse."

"You don't know which one's the Big Dipper, either, do you?" she accused him.

"Of course I do! Every Boy Scout was taught that by the age of five."

"Five? Last I heard, you had to be at least seven to be even the most junior of Scouts."

"Picky, picky. There, that's the Big Dipper over there."

Alicia tried to follow the direction of his pointing finger, but her attention kept getting waylaid by his hand, which was so close by.

"Do you see it?" he asked.

"Mmm, I see." He had an artist's hands, she dreamily decided. They were lean and strong.

"And over there is Orion's Belt."

When she turned, their noses almost bumped. He was looking at her, not at the sky. She was so close, she could see herself reflected in the dark blue of his eyes. She could also see desire. For her?

What little space there was between them was suddenly filled with heat, with a sexual radiance. Drawn to him as if he'd thrown an invisible lasso around her, she swayed closer, obeying the unspoken command of his arm around her shoulder. Then his lips touched hers and she was lost.

At the first sweet taste of her response, Mitch tightened his hand on her shoulder. His question was answered—her lips were as luscious as they looked, better than he could have imagined. He lifted both hands to curl them into the silkiness of her hair and drew her deeper into the kiss.

She was still too far away. He slid one hand down her back to gather her closer. She melted against him, her lips parting to admit his tempting tongue. He eagerly took advantage of the invitation.

Alicia was unprepared for the rush of fiery passion consuming her. She'd never felt this way before, never known she *could* feel this way. The overwhelming force of her emotions left her trembling.

As if aware of her uncertainty, Mitch gentled the kiss, moving from hungry desire to tenderness. His mouth softened on hers before slowly, regretfully lifting the slightest bit.

They stared at each other, their breaths mingling, their lips a mere heartbeat apart.

"You taste like wild strawberries," he whispered huskily.

Since her lip gloss was no doubt on his lips, she suspected he'd taste like wild strawberries, too. She was incredibly tempted to find out. Yet something held her back. She wanted to see the look in his eyes, wanted to know if she was the only one shaken by their kiss.

Her eyes slowly lifted to his. There she found a deep and quiet satisfaction without any hint of gloating. She also saw wonder and hunger. She smiled.

It was only then that Alicia realized her hands were braced on his chest. That funny *da-dum-da-dum* beneath her palm was the ragged beating of his heart. She pressed her hand against the life-giving pulse, thrilling to the feel of his warm skin beneath the thin cotton of his shirt.

"Do you know what you're getting into here, princess?"

She shook her head.

He groaned. "Lisha..." His husky drawl transformed the abbreviation of her name into a sexy endearment.

"What?"

He lowered his lips to hers, slowly erasing the meager space between them. His mouth brushed hers in the barest whisper of a kiss, a silken promise. He whispered her name again before stoically setting her away from him.

She didn't question his actions. Her own self-restraint was hanging by a shoestring, and she could tell from the slight unsteadiness of his hands, the flush on his hard cheeks, that his control was equally tenuous.

"We'd better go back," he said gruffly.

Alicia nodded, even though she had a feeling that there would be no going back, no turning away from that kiss they'd just shared.

Four

The ride back to the lodge passed in a blur as Alicia sat behind Mitch, her cheek pressed against his back. Their combined body heat warmed the soft leather of his brown bomber jacket. She didn't think she'd ever be able to smell leather again and not think of him. She wouldn't be able to view a sunset or see the stars without thinking of him.

She had it bad! She wryly acknowledged the fact. But instead of being upset by the realization, she hugged it to her like a child anticipating Christmas. She felt so breathtakingly alive, as if she were on the cutting edge of life.

She couldn't get their kiss out of her mind. When she'd first looked into his eyes, right before he'd kissed her, she'd experienced such a strong sense of destiny—as if she were gazing into her own future. He hadn't rushed her. It had been slow, inevitable and unbelievably exciting.

The return trip ended all too soon. As Alicia hopped off the bike, she had a feeling Mitch would have kissed her again had Red and her father not both been waiting on the porch when they returned.

"So, did you two have fun?" Ray asked.

Mitch hadn't been questioned by a girl's father since he was in high school. It didn't feel any better now than it had then.

"We went up to see the sunset by Pyramid Lake," Alicia replied.

"Don't tell Gloria, but I'm thinking of getting one of those motorcycles myself," Ray confessed. "Always did want one."

"You're welcome to try mine if you'd like, Ray," Mitch offered. "I'll give you a trial run."

Ray looked as if Mitch had just handed him the key to the crown jewels. "Really?"

"Sure. Tomorrow if you'd like."

"Great! But let's not tell Gloria about this."

"Let's not tell Gloria what?" the person in question asked as she came out onto the porch. "Why, good evening, Mitch."

"Ma'am." Mitch reached up to touch the brim of his Stetson in greeting before remembering he wasn't wearing the hat.

"I've just made some fresh coffee," Gloria said. "Would you like some?"

"No, thanks. I'd better get moving along. Come on, Red."

The Irish setter lifted her head and wagged her tail but made no move to obey his command. What was it with him and independently minded females all of a sudden? He whistled sharply. Red got to her feet, yawned and then ambled down to join him. "Whatever happened to blind obedience?" he muttered.

"It went the way of suits of armor and the guillotine, thank heavens," Alicia replied.

"Too bad."

"Oh, I don't know. There's something to be said for freedom—of choice and of action." It was her way of saying that she'd chosen to let him kiss her, had chosen to kiss him back.

The gleam in his blue eyes informed her that he'd received her message, loud and clear. "Now that you mention it, freedom does have a lot to recommend it," he murmured with a steamy look in her direction. "A *lot* to recommend it."

He smiled at her flustered expression before snapping his fingers for Red, who this time stood sharply at attention by his side. "Good night, all. Pleasant dreams."

Alicia didn't know about pleasant, but her dreams were certainly memorable that night. And worthy of an adults-only rating!

The next morning, Alicia was kept busy by the arrival of a group of British tourists. The tour had reserved half of the lodge's forty cabins. Most of the other cabins were already occupied with the regulars who came for a week or two each summer. By one in the afternoon, Alicia had to put up the No Vacancy sign.

What with handling special requests for roll-away beds and inquiries about where afternoon tea was served in Jasper townsite, Alicia barely had time to think. When she did, she thought about Mitch. With him working on the roof of a cabin directly across from the picture window near the front desk, it was hard not to. She saw him every time she looked up from the reservation book. There was no missing him as she pointed out allotted cabins to newcomers. She was aware of him every moment.

The photographer in her admired the symmetry of his body silhouetted against the brilliant blue sky. The woman in her just plain admired him, period. He'd stripped off his shirt, and his bronze skin gleamed in the sunlight. He remained within daydreaming distance all day.

Under those circumstances, Alicia found it hard, if not downright impossible, to concentrate. "I'm sorry. Could you please repeat the question?" she had to ask the party on the phone. "Yes, some of our cabins do come equipped with a kitchenette." Others come equipped with a rugged man on the roof, she thought with a grin and another look at Mitch. "Would you prefer a river, valley or a mountain view? A fireplace? Yes, we do have a cabin available for that date. It's for your thirtieth anniversary? Congratulations." Alicia made a note beside the reservation to put a special bouquet in the cabin. "Fine. We'll see you then."

Alicia kept her eyes on Mitch as she hung up the phone.

"Enjoying the view?"

Alicia inwardly grimaced at being caught ogling Mitch by the biggest gossip at the lodge, the biggest gossip in all of Alberta, for that matter! "Why, Mrs. Humphries. I didn't see you standing there."

"Yes, I noticed that. And I've told you before. Call me Darlene."

Darlene Humphries and her husband Dick had been coming to the Riverside Lodge for almost ten years now. Dick came for three weeks of trout fishing. Darlene came for three weeks of storytelling—her own. Every unwary new guest was regaled with the story of Darlene's life. The veteran guests knew when to take cover. Alicia usually did, too, but today Mitch had distracted her.

"How can I help you, Darlene?"

"Well, I couldn't help but notice the way you were eyeing that young man working on the roof over there," Darlene said. "Is he a friend of yours?"

"He's the handyman here at the lodge."

"Oh." Darlene looked disappointed. In her book, clearly, a mere handyman wasn't worthy of such attention. "In that case, have you seen Gloria? Don't you just love that cute little Canadian accent of hers? I think the way she says *out*—'' Darlene made it sound like *owt* ''—is just wonderful. Anyway, I was going to tell her all about my sister's gout when she had to run off to save those muffins of hers. They are delicious, you know. I had my cholesterol checked, did I tell you?''

Alicia was used to the buckshot-scattered way that Darlene's mind worked. Maintaining a conversation with her was nearly impossible. The best one could do was smile and attempt to keep up, which is what Alicia did.

"The doctor's good-looking," Darlene continued. "I told him he should come up here. He'd make a nice husband for you. He's been to the Himalayas, you know. Oh, look. There's that nice Mrs. Levitz. I think I'll go welcome her to the lodge. See you later, dear.''

Alicia heaved a sigh of relief and felt guilty for not warning poor Mrs. Levitz about the incurably curious Darlene Humphries. Not everyone coming to the lodge wanted to share confidences. In fact, many came to get away from it all. She wondered if Mitch, who disliked sharing confidences, was one of those who'd come here to escape. And if so, from what?

She looked out the window again. He was still working on the roof. Still looking good. Still making her heart beat faster.

"Still enjoying the view?" Gloria inquired with a grin.

Alicia started guiltily. Curses! Caught again!

"That's all right, dear." Gloria patted Alicia's flushed cheek. "I know how it is."

"I wish I did," Alicia muttered. There were times when she hungered for knowledge, intimate knowledge—of Mitch.

"What was that, dear?"

Alicia busied herself tidying charge receipts. "I said—you know how what is?"

"Life."

"Then tell me."

"Can't do that. You have to find out on your own. Just as I found out about this ridiculous idea of Ray's to tool around on Mitch's motorbike this afternoon."

"Does Dad know you know?"

"If he didn't before, he does now," Gloria returned, pointing at Ray, who'd just joined them from the back of the house. "I forbid it, do you hear me!" Gloria told him.

"Now, Gloria," he said placatingly, "don't go getting upset."

"I never heard of such a lame-brained idea in all my life! If anybody is going to teach you to ride a motorcycle, it'll be me," she stated, her hands on her hips. "Well, what are you two looking at me like that for? Haven't you ever met a woman who knows how to ride a motorcycle before?"

"You're kidding, right?" Alicia said.

"I've never seen you ride a bike," Ray noted in bewilderment. "When did you learn?"

"I grew up with six brothers, one of whom rides bikes for a living, or had you forgotten that fact, Ray?"

"Your brother knowing how to ride doesn't have anything to do with your knowing how to ride. Besides, we've been married all these years and I've never seen you near a motorcycle."

"You never forget how to ride a bike," Gloria loftily informed him.

"We'll talk about this later," Ray said, indicating the new guests who'd just come in to register.

"We certainly will," Gloria responded.

The discussion continued as soon as the guests left with their cabin key in hand. Alicia would have left her father and stepmother to straighten this out by themselves, but they had her hemmed in behind the front desk.

Sighing, she let her gaze stray to the picture window, only to find that Mitch was no longer on the roof. He was walking toward the lodge. Coming inside a second later, he raised his eyebrows at the sound of Ray arguing with Gloria.

Alicia could understand his surprise. Gloria was the live wire in the family. Normally Ray was the quiet dreamer. But not this afternoon. "If it's not safe for me to be on a motorbike, it's not safe for you, either!" Ray was stating with uncustomary vehemence.

"I've got a suggestion to make," Mitch inserted, having heard enough to get the gist of the problem. "Why don't the two of you take one of those brush-up courses the park district is offering in town? That way, you can learn, or relearn, how to ride a motorcycle together."

There was a moment of silence.

"I like that idea, Mitch," Gloria decided.

"You can use my bike if you need it," he offered.

"No, thanks anyway," Ray said. "Now that I know Gloria's interested, we'll go check out one of those scooters for ourselves. I saw them for sale over at the dealership. But I had no idea that Gloria here—" he tucked an arm around his wife's shoulders "—would be so receptive to the idea."

"You should have talked to me about it," she replied, giving Ray an exasperated, albeit loving, look. "It's never wise to jump to conclusions or to hide something from the one you love."

Alicia wondered if she'd imagined the disconcerted expression on Mitch's face. A blink later, it was gone. Must have been her imagination, she decided. Heaven knew it had certainly been working overtime where Mitch was concerned!

* * *

Alicia's life over the next few days continued to take on the rosy-hued overtones of a fantasy. Although Mitch's work and the steady flow of guests checking in and out of the lodge prevented Alicia from spending much time with him during the day, every evening she accompanied him on his motorbike. Each time, they drove to a different place, but it always felt the same—magical.

When she was with Mitch, she began to really believe that he cared for her, that what they had was special. And his kisses…she had yet to come up with a way to describe them. Fantastic didn't even come close!

But she wasn't merely attracted to Mitch, she was intrigued by him, as well. When she'd first met him, he'd seemed like a drifter with no roots. But the more time she spent with him, the more he slowly let her get to know him, the more convinced she was that there was so much more to the man. Beneath his easy-going exterior, she sensed a private side to him that he didn't share easily with others—a side that hinted at regret, perhaps even suffering. He'd get a certain look in his eyes, a faraway expression on his face, and she'd ache for him. But there was no way of prying the information out of him. He could be incredibly stubborn.

She also sensed a bedrock integrity in him, along with an almost old-fashioned sense of right and wrong. Indeed, Mitch could have been a throwback to those bygone years of the frontier hero, the days when a man was a man and looked out for a woman. Sometimes it was sweet. Other times, it was frustrating. And occasionally it was downright amusing. She recalled one incident in particular.

"That's no way to speak to a lady." Mitch had issued the growled warning to a guest who was loudly protesting to Alicia because "the damn pop machine is broken."

After taking one look at Mitch's rugged build, the guest had quickly made his departure.

"Bully," Alicia had affectionately teased Mitch.

"Who, me? I'm just helpin' to keep law and order, ma'am."

"You and the Mounties, eh? Do you always get your man, or your woman, as the case may be?"

"When I get my woman, *you'll* be the first to know," he had promised her in a sexy undertone accompanied by a meaningful look. "The very first."

On Monday, Mitch got the afternoon off and invited her to come with him for a picnic lunch. They were supposed to take his motorcycle, but Alicia ended up gathering so much stuff—food-filled wicker baskets, blankets and other paraphernalia—that to fit it all in, they had to take Mitch's battered pickup instead.

Like its owner, the truck had character. There were several bumper stickers on the back bumper, her favorite being the one that read If It Ain't Broke, Don't Fix It. A Denver Broncos' sign hung from the rearview mirror, and several of Red's doggy toys were strewn throughout the truck's cab. Alicia almost sat on one, a ball that squeaked.

"Just toss it in the back," Mitch told her as he started the engine, which hummed like a champ.

"I feel guilty leaving Red behind," Alicia admitted as she looked out the window at the woebegone expression on the dog's face.

"Don't. Today is just for the two of us, even though it looks like you brought enough to feed an army," he said as they pulled onto the highway.

"You're not hungry?" she countered.

"When we get to our final destination, I'll show you exactly how...hungry...I am," he promised her with a slow smile.

* * *

Their final destination turned out to be Pyramid Lake. As usual, Mitch hadn't told her where they were going ahead of time. She was delighted by his sentimental gesture. It was the first time they'd returned to the site of their first kiss.

Mitch came around to open the door, ready to assist her out of the truck the same way he'd assisted her into it. Only this time, he made the most of the fact that they were not being watched by half the guests at the lodge. Putting his hands on her waist, he lifted her from the truck but didn't set her right down. Instead, he kept her in his arms, with her feet dangling above the ground, long enough to kiss her thoroughly and enjoyably.

Even after she was back on terra firma, Alicia still felt as if she were floating in midair. Mitch had that effect on her.

"Help me spread out the blanket," she requested once she'd recovered her breath.

She quickly discovered that his idea of help was to get in the way enough to make a nuisance of himself.

"Out of the way, cowboy," she grandly commanded. "Let me show you how a woman does it."

"I'm just dyin' for you to show me how a woman does it," he drawled. "Come a little closer so I won't miss a thing."

She tossed a package of paper cups at him.

He strove to look hurt. "Did I misunderstand you, ma'am? I'm sorry. I'm just a simple mountain boy at heart."

"Right."

"I don't know many big-city women like you."

"I'll bet."

"So you're a gamblin' woman, are you? I like that. And I like this." He swooped down to steal a kiss that she was more than willing to give.

"I like this, too," she murmured against his lips, even though her feeling had long since passed from *liking* to *wanting* and was getting darn close to *needing*. That he should want her back was almost too good to be true.

The growling of one of their stomachs cut the kiss short. Each denied that their stomach would have been so gauche as to be the culprit. But by mutual agreement they began digging into the food-filled baskets Alicia had brought along.

The roast-beef sandwiches were made of paper-thin slices of tender Alberta beef on thick slabs of homemade bread— Lithuanian rye, one of Gloria's specialties. Separate airtight containers held cherry tomatoes, crisp dill pickles and corn chips. For dessert, there were slices of strawberry-rhubarb pie.

Afterward they lay replete, too stuffed to move. At least that's what Mitch claimed. But Alicia discovered that if she tickled him between his third and fourth ribs, he moved plenty. And in her direction. She was caught before she knew it, which, of course, was what she'd been hoping for.

"What are you doing?" she demanded as he tumbled her onto the blanket beside him.

"Kissing you." He put his words into action. "Can't you tell?"

"Mmm." Alicia didn't waste time with verbal communication. Instead she kissed him back with unrestrained passion. Alicia had never considered herself a passionate, sensual being. Now, thanks to Mitch, she knew better—and she wanted to discover more.

Mitch helped her on her quest, teaching her the deliciously erotic little tongue touches that could turn a simple kiss into a volcanic furnace. She repeated what she'd learned, elaborating and adding new twists of her own.

When his hands tugged the hem of her shirt from her jeans, she returned the favor. He always wore blue cham-

bray work shirts. And she always loved the way he looked
in them. Of course, she loved the way he looked out of them
even better.

Apparently Mitch felt the same way about her attire because moments later, his fingers were unsteadily sliding her
opened shirt from her shoulders. She murmured her impatience, then sighed with pleasure as his lips feathered over
her bare skin, caressing her collarbone.

When his kisses lowered to the creamy slope of her breast,
she was a goner. The things he did to her with his tongue
made her shiver in delight. She'd never known such reckless excitement.

When she finally got his shirt open, she slid her hands
around to his back, tugging him to her. The sheerness of her
bra provided no protection against the tempting abrasion of
his hair-covered chest. Her fingers dug into his waist as she
nibbled on his ear, whispering her pleasure.

He reached for her, but instead of her warm flesh, he felt
something else. His fingers closed around it. His wallet. It
must have dropped out of his pocket during their earlier
tussle. In it, was a reminder of the secret he'd been keeping
from Alicia. He had to tell her now, while he still could, before it was too late.

As much as Mitch wanted to keep her in his loving arms,
he slowly withdrew them and pulled away. The sultry look
in her expressive brown eyes almost made him forget his
good intentions.

"We need to talk," he said in a strained voice. "There's
something I've been meaning to tell you." He fingered his
wallet and broodingly stared off into the distance, as if
hoping to find the future laid out there.

She knew from his voice that something was wrong. Sitting up, she hurriedly rebuttoned her blouse. "What is it?"
she asked, laying her hand on his arm.

"You remember asking about that four-leaf clover I carry in here?"

Alicia frowned, failing to see what that could possibly have to do with anything.

"Do you remember?" he repeated.

She nodded.

"My daughter gave it to me," he said bluntly. "She's flying in tomorrow to spend the summer with me."

With his words, Alicia's rosy fantasy world came crashing down around her unsuspecting ears. She felt as if she'd stepped into glacier water. Chilled to the bone, she withdrew from him. "You've . . . got . . . a daughter?"

"That's right."

"I see." She certainly did see, even though she didn't want to. She saw that there was another reason for his interest in her—an all-too-familiar reason. Mitch hadn't been making love to her because he'd wanted to, but because it had been expedient to do so.

It had happened to her before. Rob's words came back to haunt her. *She'll be home taking care of the kids. Why else do you think I'm going with her?* Why else, indeed? How could she have fallen for the same old ploy again? It had all been a pipe dream—one that had turned into a painful nightmare.

"So . . . you have a daughter," she said carefully, as if the words might cut her. And, indeed, she felt ripped apart inside. "Do you have a wife, as well?"

"I have an *ex*-wife," he clarified with emphatic anger. "I've been divorced for four years. What do you think? That I've got the little family stashed away someplace while I fool around up here in the mountains with you?"

"It's certainly within the realm of possibility."

"No, it's not!" he shot back, infuriated by her insinuation. "I wouldn't do that."

"How am I supposed to know that?" she inquired coldly.

"You're supposed to know *me*."

"I thought I was beginning to," she muttered, "but clearly I was mistaken." She turned away from him, determined not to let him see how shattered she was. She took a moment to put her emotions in the deep freeze, to regain some kind of control. "Why didn't you tell me you had a daughter?"

"I've been meaning to...."

"I'll bet."

"The right moment never came up."

"The hell it didn't!" she exploded, her resolution to stay cool and calm forgotten. "What about the time you talked about my being good with kids? I would have thought that would have been the perfect opportunity." His comment took on an entirely new meaning in light of his own parenthood. Just when she began believing that he was interested in her for herself, he dropped this on her.

"I knew you'd take it like this," he muttered.

"Like what?"

"Misunderstand."

"Oh, I understand just fine. It's perfectly clear. You've got a daughter who just so happens to be coming for the summer. And let me guess...it just so happens that you don't have a baby-sitter for your daughter while you're working. And since I'm so good with children, you figured I could help out, right?"

"Wrong."

"So you've already made other baby-sitting arrangements for her?"

He didn't answer.

"I knew it," she said.

"You don't know anything except what you've convinced yourself in your own mind! It's got nothing to do with reality."

"The reality is that your daughter is coming tomorrow and you haven't made any plans for that occurrence. What are you going to do with her while you're working?"

"That's my problem."

"It's everyone's problem if you just leave her the way that couple left that poor little boy in the car."

"I'd never do that to my daughter!" he shouted.

"Then what will you do?"

"We'll manage just fine without your help."

"Do my dad and Gloria know about your daughter coming?"

"I told them, yes."

"Why didn't they tell me?"

"I asked them not to. I said I'd be telling you about her myself."

"Well, you've certainly done that at the last possible minute."

"Because I knew you wouldn't understand. I was all set to tell you about Nicole that first time we came out to Pyramid Lake, but then you started talking about being taken for granted as a baby-sitter and how that was an occupational hazard."

"It is! I would think this situation is a prime example."

"Damn it, I never asked you to help me with Nicole!"

"That would be pretty hard to do considering I didn't know about her. But that would have been the next step. This isn't the first time something like this has happened to me, you know. No, this has got an all-too-familiar ring to it. 'Be nice to the little librarian for a few days, and then she'll take your kid off your hands.' "

"Nicole has nothing to do with me spending time with you," he ground out. "Just because some jerk messed up in the past doesn't mean that I had the same plan in mind. You can't judge all men by the actions of one."

"I don't judge *all* men. Just those with children. Especially those with children they don't tell me about until the last minute." So much for his bedrock integrity, she reflected bitterly. What a fool she'd been.

"And if I had told you about Nicole, would it have made any difference?"

Her expression was answer enough.

"See, it wouldn't have made any difference. You'd have jumped to the same illogical conclusion then." He shook his head. "I'd hoped that you'd know me better than to think I'd pull something underhanded like that."

"Lying about having a daughter sounds pretty underhanded to me."

"I didn't lie!"

"In my book, omission is equal to lying."

"Then why did you omit telling me about this man in your past? The one who's left you so spooked."

"There's nothing that says I have to tell you my life story," she retorted.

"Exactly."

"But having a daughter is different. That is something current. Something relevant."

"And I'd say, judging by your reaction right now, that whatever that guy did to you is still current, still relevant. It's certainly still clouding your judgment."

"My judgment is just fine! Yours is way off base if you think I can't see the writing on the wall!"

"You can't see anything, you're so blinded with prejudice."

"Right. And I suppose you expect me to believe that you were swept off your feet by my beauty," she said sarcastically.

"No. I don't expect you to believe that."

"Good." She ruthlessly stifled the pain caused by his words. "Because I wouldn't."

"It was your voice and your eyes that got me, plus your warmth and your passion for life."

"You've got a way with words," she choked out. "I'll grant you that."

"Oh, come on," he muttered with frustration. "Get real here! Since when have I been a smooth talker?"

"Desperate men say desperate things."

"And desperate women don't know what the hell they're talking about! You really want to know why I've spent time with you? Well, this is a hint!"

Mitch yanked her into his arms and kissed her. He'd completely lost patience with her, and his kiss informed her of that fact. It was filled with a passion dominated by anger. Had it continued that way, Alicia would have had no trouble remaining as cool as a marble statue. But instead, his anger quickly turned to wooing desire, and suddenly she was struggling not to let herself go.

She wouldn't give in. She couldn't! She'd been hurt before, but that pain was nothing compared to the heartache Mitch could cause her. For in the end, she still wasn't entirely convinced, despite his fiery words and kisses, that Mitch was telling her the truth. He'd lied to her before. How did she know he wasn't lying to her now?

And so she managed the control necessary, and while she may have softened momentarily, her defenses were firmly back in place once he ended the kiss as abruptly as he'd begun it.

"Can you honestly look me in the eye and tell me that you didn't think I could help with your daughter at all?" she demanded.

The flash of discomfiture in his blue eyes was momentary, but Alicia saw it. "I knew it."

"Naturally, I hoped the two of you would get along," he said defensively. "What's wrong with that?"

"I'd rather not travel this route again, Mitch," she replied wearily.

"But you haven't even met Nicole."

"I don't have to meet her to know that I want more out of life than just being a baby-sitter. Now, are you going to drive me home, or am I going to have to hitch a ride?"

"I'll take you back," he growled, "since it's obvious you're in no mood to listen to reason."

The only thing obvious to Alicia was that not only was their picnic over, but so was their so-called relationship. Her trust in Mitch had been badly damaged, and there was no telling if it could ever be repaired.

Five

"I'm sorry I haven't been spending as much time with you and Dad as I should have," Alicia told Gloria as she helped her stepmother with the next day's batch of maple-bran muffins. "But all that's going to change now."

"Now that you're angry with Mitch, you mean," Gloria said.

Startled, Alicia almost spilled the syrup she was pouring into the bowl of muffin batter. "How did you know that I'm angry with him?"

"The fact that you didn't speak one word to him yesterday or this morning sort of gave you away."

"He's got a daughter, you know," Alicia stated, picking up a wooden spoon and stirring the mixture for all she was worth—which, at that moment, didn't feel like a whole heck of a lot.

"Yes, I know he has a daughter. He's gone to pick her up at Edmonton airport."

"Why is it that men always think I'd be so good at looking after their kids?" Alicia demanded.

"Because you would be," Gloria calmly replied, taking the spoon away from Alicia before she did any further damage.

"Did it ever bother you that dad had two children when you met him? Did you ever wonder—"

"If he was looking for a second mother for them? The thought did cross my mind once or twice, but you know I don't think it really ever occurred to your father. He just wanted us all to get along. Men tend to see things in simpler terms than we women do. To them things are black-and-white, while to us they are infinite shades of gray."

"They get the better end of the deal," Alicia noted darkly.

"I don't know, dear. I'm not saying we're the only ones with doubts. There must be plenty of men out there who wonder if they're being married for themselves or for their ability to provide security to a woman and her children."

"Her children, his children, their children. It's messy, isn't it?"

"It can be, yes. But it can also be wonderfully rewarding. You and your brother have certainly enriched my life, even if there were times when I wondered if your brother was trying to *shorten* it. Dropping water balloons on me from his second-story bedroom window just about every time I stepped out onto the back porch, do you remember?"

Alicia nodded.

"Much as I tried, your brother never quite felt that he belonged anywhere," Gloria said sadly. "I hope Mitch's daughter doesn't feel that way."

"Do you know what arrangements Mitch has made for her care?" Alicia asked, trying to sound nonchalant.

"I offered my help, but he turned me down."

The news surprised Alicia. "He did?"

"Yes. He said he wanted to spend time with her himself, that he wanted her with him. And he said he didn't want to impose on me that way. As if I'd offer if it were an imposition."

"You'd offer. You're a sucker for lost causes."

"Look who's talking," Gloria retorted. "You'd have offered, too, if you hadn't gotten burned."

But Alicia had been burned, and she couldn't forget the doubts. The problem was that she couldn't forget Mitch, either.

Although Alicia tried to stay out of the way for Mitch's arrival with his daughter, as luck would have it, she was outside talking with some guests when his pickup truck pulled in. The first view she got of Nicole was of a pair of shiny white shoes and brilliant polka-dot ankle socks. Alicia watched, helpless to prevent history from repeating itself, as the dainty little foot ended up in a giant-sized mud puddle.

"You were supposed to wait for Daddy to help you," Alicia heard Mitch gently say to the little girl. She'd never heard him use that tone of voice before—it was like a hug wrapped up in a husky baritone.

Alicia saw the quivering of Nicole's bottom lip, saw the rapid blinking to avoid tears. The child's outfit, polka-dot leggings and top in neon yellow and black, looked like something out of a trendy fashion catalogue. With her moussed hair styled and sprayed into vertical spikes, Nicole looked more like a miniature version of an adult than a child. Even the little girl's damp eyes held a cynicism beyond her years. "I don't care," she stated belligerently. "I hated these shoes anyway!"

"Come on, we'll go clean you up," Mitch said with quiet patience.

What was it about the sight of a man with a little girl in his arms that was so touching? Alicia wondered. What was it about watching a man being a daddy that made you want to hug him? Particularly *this* man, the solitary loner with an apparently huge soft spot for his little girl.

Remember your speech about getting tough, Alicia silently lectured herself. *Remember you're not going to be a patsy again. You're not going to melt with emotion. You're going to keep your distance.*

She soon found keeping her resolutions wasn't as easy as it sounded. For one thing, Nicole was a real heartbreaker. Without the hair mousse, her midnight-dark hair fell into a smooth pageboy. She had Mitch's blue eyes. But it was the bewildered, wary expression in those young eyes that so reminded Alicia of herself at that age. She knew how it felt to be shuttled between two households. Even in the best of situations, it was hard on a child. She could see it was hard on Nicole.

Alicia once again reminded herself that she was no longer going to be the world's caretaker. She repeated it a thousand times as she helped out around the lodge, pitching in wherever she was needed, doing more than her share of the work over the next few days because she didn't want to think about Mitch or his appealing daughter.

She'd even taken to helping the maids clean out the cabins. But Alicia's mind was not on her work as she stripped sheets from beds and stuffed them in a large white laundry bag. Actually, she felt as if her mind had checked out for the day.

Lost in thought, Alicia stepped off the cabin's porch, only to be almost knocked off her feet by a three-foot torpedo in the form of a child. The laundry bag fell to the ground, and so did the child. It was Nicole. Alicia immediately knelt down beside her.

"Are you all right?"

The little girl blinked away tears as she nodded stoically. "Don't tell Daddy I was running," Nicole said. "I promised I'd be good."

Up close, Alicia was struck by how similar Nicole's eyes really were to Mitch's. They even had the same navy-blue ring around the lighter blue iris. They also held the same flashes of loneliness that, once displayed, were quickly shielded.

"It was just an accident," Alicia softly reassured the little girl. "No harm done, except to those knees of yours. Why don't you come on inside the lodge so we can fix you up?"

Nicole looked horrified at the idea. "I don't want to be fixed! That's what Daddy did to Red, and now she can't have puppies!"

Alicia tried not to laugh. "I meant we'd clean up your knees and put something on them so they won't get infected. I won't fix you the way Red's been fixed, I promise," she stated solemnly.

"I don't know. My daddy says I'm not supposed to go anywheres with strangers."

"That's good advice. But I'm not a stranger. I live over there in the lodge."

Nicole still looked suspicious. "A nice lady called Gloria lives there. She's got gray hair and bakes good cookies and stuff."

"I live there with Gloria. My name is Alicia. Gloria is my stepmom, and she does bake good cookies and stuff. In fact, she's in the kitchen now making chocolate-chip cookies. We'll go see her if you like. Maybe she'll let us have one."

"Can I ride in the go-mobile?"

Alicia wondered what a "go-mobile" was until she saw Nicole expectantly eyeing the golf cart used for transporting laundry, among other things. "Sure. Hop in. But hold on tight. No standing up."

"Okay."

Five minutes later, Nicole was sitting at the pine table in the lodge's large homey kitchen—her knee bandaged and a warm cookie in her hand.

"Feel better now?" Alicia asked her.

Nicole nodded. "You get to live here all the time?" she asked around a mouthful of cookie.

"Just during the summer," Alicia replied.

"Me, too. Just for the summer. Maybe."

"Maybe?"

Nicole shrugged. "My mom gets to decide where I stay."

"And where would you stay if you got to decide?" Alicia couldn't resist asking.

"Here with the cookies," Nicole said pragmatically.

"Gloria, have you seen . . . ?" Mitch's concerned voice dropped off as he found Nicole. He frowned. "What's going on here?"

"Nothing dramatic," Alicia replied, very much aware that this was the first time she'd spoken to Mitch in four days. Trust her to be wearing her oldest pair of jeans, the ones with the hole in the left knee. But at least her pink-and-white-striped seersucker blouse was new and relatively flattering. "We're taking a cookie break."

"Come on, kiddo." Mitch held out his hand to his daughter. "I told you not to bother them here at the lodge."

"She's not bothering us," Alicia protested.

"What happened to her knee?" Mitch demanded in concern, having just caught sight of the bandage.

"Just a little accident. She'll be fine," Alicia assured him. "No harm done."

"I wasn't naughty, Daddy." Nicole turned to Alicia for confirmation. "Tell him I wasn't."

"She wasn't naughty," Alicia dutifully repeated. "It was just an accident. You know how those happen," she said with a meaningful look in Mitch's direction.

"Yeah, right. I just hope a Frisbee wasn't involved."

"No, not this time."

"That's reassuring. For a minute there I thought the mad Frisbee launcher was on the loose again."

The brief look he gave Alicia spoke of shared times, shared laughter. Then it was gone. She mourned its passing. Now he looked as stiff and unapproachable as a bull moose.

"Well, come on, kiddo," Mitch told his daughter. "Time to go."

"Go where?" Nicole asked.

"Back outside."

"Aw, do I have to, Daddy?"

"Yes, you have to."

"How come?"

"'Cause I said so."

Nicole got a mutinous expression on her face. "But I want to stay."

"You've stayed long enough."

"Let her stay," Alicia said. "She's not bothering anyone."

"She certainly isn't," Gloria concurred. "I've told you before that Nicole is welcome to visit any time either you or she would like."

"Thanks," Mitch said, "but we can manage on our own."

"But we don't have cookies like this at your house, Daddy," Nicole pointed out.

"Mitch, can I talk to you outside for a moment, please?" Alicia requested, deciding it was time to take the bull by the horns, so to speak.

For a moment she thought he was going to refuse. Instead, he pivoted and stalked outside.

"What is it?" he demanded impatiently.

"Why are you being so stubborn about Nicole coming over to the lodge?" Alicia asked.

"I don't want her becoming a nuisance," he said stiffly. "And I don't want you becoming a baby-sitter."

"I don't mind."

"That's not what you were saying the other day. And I've got no intention of having you accuse me of taking advantage of your generosity. Because, believe me, if I wanted to take advantage of your generosity, I'd do it in ways that had nothing to do with baby-sitting and everything to do with..." His heated gaze focused on her mouth, visually completing the sentence.

Alicia took a deep breath, feeling as if he'd actually touched her even though he hadn't moved an inch. "All right, I'll admit I may have misjudged you...."

"'May have'!"

"Maybe you weren't really trying to con me into looking after Nicole. I'm willing to give you the benefit of the doubt in this case."

"How generous of you!" he growled. "Not good enough."

"What do you mean, 'not good enough'?"

"What I said. You can keep your offers to yourself."

His anger diffused her own. "Why are you being so pigheaded about this?" she demanded in exasperation. "Don't you want what's best for Nicole?"

"Of course I do."

"Then accept the offer to help. It doesn't just come from me. It comes from Gloria, as well."

"How do I know you're not going to change your mind tomorrow and act all imposed upon?" he retorted.

"Because I don't feel imposed upon." And she didn't. Not anymore. "Look, someone who's planning on taking advantage of me wouldn't keep refusing my offer to help."

"Unless they're very clever," he pointed out.

"Which isn't the case here," she returned with a grin.

Tipping his hat back with the tip of his thumb, Mitch eyed her with equal parts of suspicion and amusement. "What is this? Some new feminine trick of yours where you convince a man to agree with you by insulting his intelligence?"

"I don't know any feminine tricks."

"Right." His expression was patently disbelieving. "What about those blatant looks you gave me when I was working on the roof last week?"

"I did no such thing," Alicia denied, although, indeed, she had.

"You most certainly did. And I wasn't the only one to notice. Darlene Humphries took great joy in scolding me for distracting you from your duties."

"Well, if you're going to believe *her*..."

"Hello, Mrs. Humphries," Mitch said over Alicia's shoulder, causing Alicia to turn around guiltily.

There was no one there. "Very funny," she muttered.

"Just tell me one thing, and no fibs this time. Is this your way of declaring a truce between us?"

"I suppose it is."

"Why?" he demanded bluntly.

"Because I don't like fighting with you."

"What *do* you like doing with me?" he softly asked.

Kissing you, hugging you, touching you... Alicia's mind reeled with the possibilities of that question. He was watching her, and she felt the warm speculation of his gaze as vividly as a caress.

She looked away from him before those deep blue eyes of his tempted her to reveal more than she should. "I liked watching the sunset with you," she said in a deliberately casual voice. "You should take Nicole out to see it someday."

"I already have. In fact, I thought I'd take her to Maligne Lake on my next day off. I've heard it's supposed to be pretty over there."

"It's beautiful there. One of the most scenic places in the Rockies, or in the world, for that matter."

"Not that you're prejudiced, of course," he teased her.

"Of course not."

Their gazes collided, and this time there was no looking away. Alicia was well and truly caught, drawn in by the unspoken desire in his eyes and the force of her own attraction to him.

"Since you're the expert, maybe you should come along and share your knowledge with us," Mitch suggested.

"My knowledge, eh?"

"That's right. Unlimited photo stops," he promised her with a slow smile.

"Oh, well, in that case . . . how can I say no?"

"It's a date, then. This Monday morning at ten. Be ready."

Alicia tried to be ready, but there was no way she could be prepared for the exhilaration she felt at being in Mitch's company once again. She'd waffled over what to wear for at least two hours, an unusual occurrence for her. In the end, she'd chosen the casual-but-together look of her best pair of jeans, an oversize white T-shirt and a warm fuchsia cardigan sweater.

It felt good to be with Mitch again, to be sharing the sunshine and the fresh air with him, not to mention the close quarters of the pickup's bench front seat.

"Are we there yet?" Nicole kept asking from the compact back seat, which she shared with the affectionate Irish setter. "Red wants to know."

"Not yet. I'll let Red know when we get there," Mitch said each of the ten times she asked.

"Maligne Canyon," Mitch read aloud as they passed the road sign. "Is it worth stopping for?"

"If you like waterfalls, it is," Alicia replied.

"I think both Red and Nicole could use the break," Mitch noted dryly as his daughter piped up with another, "Daddy, are we there yet?"

"There's nothing here," Nicole complained once they'd parked and gotten out of the truck.

"There's a walk down to the waterfall," Alicia said. "Listen and you can hear the rushing water."

The walk was a short one. As they approached the waterfall, Alicia noticed the way Nicole kept shying away from the fencing along the canyon's edge.

"You go on ahead," Alicia told Mitch, who had an eager Red at the end of a leash. "I've got something in my shoe. I'll catch up with you."

"Me, too," Nicole hurriedly stated.

"All right," Mitch replied, "but don't take all day, you two slowpokes."

When Alicia sat down on a nearby boulder, Nicole quickly sat beside her and pretended to look in her shoe for a nonexistent pebble. Alicia knew because she was doing the same thing herself. There was nothing in her own shoe, either. She'd only stopped to give Nicole the opportunity to tell her what was wrong.

"Are you afraid of heights?" Alicia prompted.

Nicole shook her head and then her shoe, running her finger inside with intense concentration.

"It's okay if you are."

"It's not okay to be afraid. It's dumb," Nicole stated.

"Says who?"

"Says my mom. She told me so when I saw this movie where monsters came out of the water."

Alicia frowned over the name of the movie. She'd seen it herself, and it certainly hadn't been intended for children. "Your mom let you see that?"

Nicole shrugged. "We have cable. She lets me see whatever I want. She doesn't mind. She says it's dumb to be scared."

Dumb possibly, but very human, Alicia thought to herself, furious at Nicole's mother for being so unfeeling. "Everybody gets scared sometimes."

"Not me. I don't even sleep with a nightlight," she bragged. "Or my teddy bear anymore. That stuff's just for kids."

Alicia's heart ached. For what was Nicole if not a "kid"? A little girl trying so hard to cover up her fears. But despite Nicole's bravado, there was no mistaking the cautious looks she kept darting toward the edge of the limestone gorge.

"There are no monsters in this water," Alicia softly assured her, "but you don't have to look if you don't want to."

"I'm not scared of monsters. I'd just sic Red on them. It's awfully loud, though, isn't it?" Nicole said.

"It's the water that's loud, not any monsters."

"How do you know?"

"I've been here before."

"Maybe the monsters were just sleeping then. I don't like loud noises."

Alicia didn't push her. "We won't go any closer to the waterfall, then. We'll just stay here until your dad and Red come back. Does that sound like a good idea to you?"

Nicole nodded her agreement. "I thought we were going to a lake. Are there going to be loud noises there, too?"

"No. Just the noise of the boat's engines."

Satisfied with the answer, Nicole refastened her gym shoe. "That's okay, then."

* * *

At Maligne Lake, before heading for the crowded boat dock, they left Red with a friend of Alicia's who worked at the lakeside gift shop.

"Why can't Red come with us?" Nicole asked.

"Because dogs aren't allowed on the boat," Mitch said.

"And because Red would rather stay and play with the other dogs," Alicia added.

"Oh." Nicole nodded solemnly. "That way Red won't get lonely, right?"

Alicia suspected that Nicole knew all about loneliness. So did Mitch. It made her want to cry. "That's right. Red won't be lonely."

"Good." With the resiliency of a six-year-old, Nicole skipped on ahead, all worries about Red apparently forgotten.

"Your little girl is lovely," one of the women in line told Alicia after Mitch had taken Nicole over to get a closer look at the incoming boat.

"Thank you, but . . ." At the last moment Alicia opted against correcting the woman. "Thank you."

"How old is she? Five?"

"Six." *But she's not mine. He's not mine, either. Unfortunately.* Alicia had never considered herself to be the possessive type, but applying the word *mine* to Mitch and Nicole was surprisingly tempting.

Careful, she warned herself. Don't get hooked on this fantasy. It's just a day's excursion. Nothing more than that.

"Keep your feet on the ground," she muttered to herself.

"That's a strange thing to say as you're just about to get on a boat," Mitch whispered in her ear. "Having second thoughts?"

"Of course not."

"Good."

His breath feathered across her temple. Had she imagined it, or had he kissed her? The smile on his face said he'd never tell.

"Where's Nicole?" she asked breathlessly.

"She's over there doing her *Rocky* routine on the steps."

"Where does she get the energy?"

"Beats me."

"How long is she staying?"

He gave her a quizzical look. "Trying to get rid of her already?"

"Not at all. I put that badly. I meant that I hope the two of you will get to spend plenty of time together." Alicia knew from her own experience that the first week or two of a child's visit were spent getting reacquainted, while the last week or two were spent emotionally preparing for the separation. For a visit to be a success, more time was needed between arrival and departure. "Does she get to spend the entire summer with you, until the end of August?"

"She's supposed to, but it rarely works out that way. My ex-wife has a way of sabotaging the visitation schedule. In fact, for a while there, I wasn't sure Nicole would be coming at all. But then Iris's buying trip to the Far East was moved up and…" Mitch deliberately relaxed his tensed jaw. Just talking about his ex-wife was enough to drive him nuts. "The important thing is that Nicole is finally here."

"I'm sorry. I didn't mean to pry."

"I wouldn't have told you if I didn't want you to know."

"Yes, I realize that," she returned. "Not telling me things you don't want me to know is a problem with you."

"I'm working on that."

"I'm glad to hear it."

"Daddy, Daddy! Is that the boat we get to go on?" Nicole asked eagerly as a tour boat neared the dock.

"That's the one," Mitch replied.

Seeing the way Nicole was fidgeting, Alicia leaned down and whispered a question in her ear, at which time Nicole nodded.

"Here, hold my camera," Alicia told Mitch, shoving it into his hands. There was no time for niceties; the boat was leaving soon.

Startled, Mitch called out after them. "Hey, where are you two going?"

"Bathroom stop," Alicia replied over her shoulder.

"Oh." He looked at the amused faces in the surrounding crowd and tried not to look as disconcerted as he felt. "Right."

He didn't relax until their return. Nor did he get on the boat. Luckily they didn't take long.

"Thanks," he muttered.

"No problem," Alicia said as she rejoined him in line.

"I should've thought of that myself. Sometimes it feels like I'm still trying to get the hang of this parenting stuff."

"I'd say you're doing pretty well," she told him.

They shared a smile before being distracted by Nicole. "I want to hold my own ticket," she said.

"All right," Mitch agreed. "But don't lose it."

"I won't," the little girl promised.

After getting on board the boat, the feminist part of Alicia was pleased to note that all the boat's crew members were female. However, the cautious part of her was a bit nervous at hearing that they were training a new woman at the helm today. But the departure was smooth as they left the dock behind and headed out.

"Welcome aboard," their guide said over the boat's loudspeaker system. "Today we're going to show you some of the most beautiful scenery in the world."

"See," Alicia whispered to Mitch. "I'm not the only one who says so."

The tour guide continued. "Maligne Lake, pronounced Ma-leen, is named after the river that feeds it. Legend has it that the Maligne River got its name from a French trapper who cursed it after almost drowning in its rapids when his boat overturned. *Maligne* in French means cunning or having an evil disposition, so the description fit as far as he was concerned."

"I can think of a few guests at the lodge that also fit that description," Mitch noted for Alicia's ears only.

"Our tour will take approximately two hours and will give you plenty of picture-taking opportunities," the guide stated.

Knowing how spectacular the views along the way were, Alicia had her camera ready. The clear, sunny weather couldn't have been better. Using her telephoto lens, she zoomed in on the glaciers clinging to the mountain peaks— they'd always reminded her of diamond tiaras adorning a monarch's head. Inspired by the play of light on solid rock and ice, she finished an entire roll of film in less than five minutes.

"They look like ice castles in the sky," Nicole said, pointing to the mountains.

"They do, don't they," Alicia agreed.

Lower down, those "ice castles" were covered with a dense forest that spread right to the very edge of the lake. That forested area, accessible only by canoeing or hiking in, was frequented by hungry bears, looking for food. Knowing that a bear can run as fast as a racehorse, Alicia had never felt the desire to go exploring in their territory. No picture was worth being chased by four hundred pounds of grumpy grizzly!

But here on the boat, she had the best of both worlds, being able to see the scenery without bothering any bears.

"Maligne Lake is the largest lake in the Canadian Rockies," the guide said. "We're heading for Spirit Island now.

Be sure and save some of your film, because the view from the island is world-famous for its beauty. When we get there, we'll give you all a chance to get off, stretch your legs and get some spectacular shots.''

Having reloaded her camera, Alicia was too busy taking pictures to really absorb the rest of the presentation. The reflection of a red canoe in the still waters looked particularly beautiful through her telephoto lens. So did a closeup shot of Nicole sitting on her father's lap.

"I'll give you a copy if it turns out okay," Alicia told Mitch, catching the inquiring look he gave her.

"Thanks." That hadn't occurred to Mitch. Actually, he'd been wondering why she'd taken his picture in the first place. For artistic or for personal reasons? Did it mean she really had gotten over her initial distrust?

Despite what she might think, Mitch wasn't accustomed to having a woman along when he was with his daughter— or having his daughter along when he was with a woman, for that matter. It was a strange feeling; strange in a good sort of way, though. This he could get used to. Very easily. Did Alicia feel the same way?

"Having fun?" he asked her.

She nodded. "This is great. How about you two?"

"Great," he murmured, warmed by the honesty of her smile. The lipstick she'd started out with was long gone. Now the sweet rose color of her lips was entirely natural. Bare. Mitch liked the image. He wanted to see more of her that way.

Nicole bouncing on his lap jogged his thoughts back to the present family outing.

"Do your horsy act, Daddy."

Mitch obligingly bounced her up and down, grateful for the chance to expend a little energy. His body needed a distraction.

Alicia watched as Nicole giggled with delight. She shared their laughter, their smiles. She felt a part of it all. A family unit.

She told herself not to get too used to the feeling because comforting as it might be, it wasn't reality. Nicole wasn't *her* daughter, and Mitch wasn't *her* husband.

But as she sat next to them on the boat, it was hard not to be drawn in by the appealing warmth of the fantasy. And when Nicole slipped her little hand in her larger one, no amount of common sense could stop Alicia from caring.

"Where's the magic?" Nicole wanted to know once they were ashore on Spirit Island, where they'd been promised a ten-minute stop. "The lady on the boat said there was magic here."

"That's what the Indians believed," Alicia said.

"Then where is it?"

"You can't see magic," Alicia pointed out as they followed the path along the hillside.

"Does that mean there's no magician living here?"

"What do you think?" Alicia returned.

"That I have to go to the bathroom again," Nicole stated.

Mitch looked panic stricken.

"But I can hold it till we get back," Nicole assured them.

Mitch heaved a sigh of relief. "Good." There were no facilities here or on the boat, either, for that matter.

The return boat ride had them arriving back at the dock too quickly for Alicia, who used up two more rolls of film, but just in time for Nicole, who raced with Alicia to the bathroom.

The combination of the fresh air and all the activity tired the little girl out to such an extent that she fell asleep on the way home. So did Red.

Enjoy Four Silhouette Sensations plus a cuddly Teddy and extra Mystery Gift

▲ Absolutely Free! ▲

We're inviting you to discover why the Silhouette Sensation series has become so popular with our readers.

Here's a truly sensational FREE offer.

We'd love you to become a regular reader of Sensations and discover just why these modern love stories with a twist in the 'tale' have become such a popular series. As a welcome we'd like you to have four Silhouette Sensations, a cuddly Teddy and a Mystery Gift ABSOLUTELY FREE.

Then, each month you can look forward to receiving four brand new Sensations, delivered to your door, postage and packing FREE! Plus our FREE Newsletter full of author news, competitions and special offers.

Turn the page for details of how to claim your free gifts!

Reader Service
FREEPOST
P.O. Box 236
Croydon
Surrey CR9 9EL

SEND NO MONEY NOW

FREE BOOKS COUPON

Yes Please rush me my four FREE SENSATIONS and two FREE GIFTS! Please also reserve me a Reader Service Subscription. If I decide not to subscribe, I shall write to you within 10 days. If I decide to subscribe I can look forward to receiving four brand new Silhouette Sensations, each month, for just £6.60 (postage and packing free). I may cancel or suspend my subscription at any time. I can keep any free books and gifts whatever I decide. I am over 18 years of age.   6S1SS

Mrs/Miss/Mr _____

Address _____

_____

_____ Postcode _____

Signature _____

Before Mitch carried Nicole from the truck, he turned to Alicia and kissed her—just once and not for long. It was enough. Her heart raced and she forgot to breathe.

He leaned back and smiled. Touching his finger to her flushed cheek, he whispered, "We'll do this again."

She knew he was right. They would do this again—kiss again, spend time together again, pretend to be a family. But was it wise? Or was she leaving herself wide open to be hurt all over again?

Six

____

"Julie, I need advice," Alicia told her best friend the second Julie answered the phone the next morning.

"Hello to you, too," Julie returned.

"I mean it. I'm in serious trouble here."

"Is it bad enough to need chocolate?"

"Yes."

"Oh-oh. This does sound bad. I'll eat the chocolate, you tell me the problem."

"It's sort of complicated," Alicia said.

"Man trouble usually is."

"How did you know it involves a man?"

"I've known you twenty years. I know the tone of voice you use when it's man trouble. So go on, tell me."

"Mitch has a daughter."

"Oh-oh."

"Exactly."

"What's she like?"

"She's great. She's just turned six, and she's got such sad eyes—"

"You're hooked," Julie noted.

"I'm not hooked. Not yet. But it's getting close."

"And that's the complication?"

"There are a number of them. First, Mitch didn't tell me anything about Nicole until the night before she arrived."

"Mistake number one. How'd you react to that?" Julie asked.

"Not well. I felt like I was being used again. I mean, here he'd been paying all this attention to me and I thought it was because he was interested in me, but then when I found out about Nicole, I thought it was because of her. See what I mean?"

"It gets more complicated than this? Wait, I need more chocolate." There was a pause, then a crunching noise before Julie mumbled, "Okay, go on."

"Mitch and I fought. I thought it was all over, whatever *it* was. But it wasn't. Nicole came, and I couldn't resist offering to help out. Only Mitch stubbornly refused that suggestion. I actually had to convince him to accept my help."

"Maybe he was just being clever, refusing so you'd offer."

"He suggested that he might be doing something like that."

"And what did you say?"

"That he wasn't clever enough to do that."

Julie laughed. "You've got a real way with men, Alicia. I'll bet he didn't appreciate that one bit."

"Actually, he smiled." Alicia's voice softened. "He's got such a nice smile."

"Maybe there's hope for the guy after all."

"What should I do?" Alicia asked.

"About what?"

"He's suggested that we go out together again."

"Wait, you skipped over something. What do you mean by *again?*" Julie demanded.

"Mitch, Nicole and I went over to Maligne Lake yesterday. We had a good time, and afterward Mitch said that we should do it again."

"And what did you say?"

"Nothing."

"That's not like you, Alicia."

"Very funny. I didn't know what to say. I feel as though I'm on a roller coaster with Mitch—one day I think he likes me, the next day I think he's just trying to use me, then I don't think that anymore. I'm so confused!"

"Do *you* like *him?*"

"I either like him a lot or I'm infuriated with him. It seems to fluctuate between the two on a daily basis."

"And today?" Julie prompted.

"I like him a lot."

"How about the day you spent with him at Maligne Lake?"

"I liked him a lot."

"Sounds to me as though you like him more often than you're infuriated with him. And you probably wouldn't be so infuriated with him in the first place if you didn't like him so much."

"You know, you could be right," Alicia said slowly.

"Of course I'm right. Chocolate always makes me wonderfully insightful. Also makes me gain weight, unfortunately, so that's all the advice I can give you today."

"Thanks, you've been a real pal."

When Mitch stopped by the front desk later that day and asked Alicia if she'd be interested in an excursion to the Columbia Icefields next week, she said yes.

Unfortunately their conversation was overheard by Darlene Humphries. The moment Mitch was gone, Darlene left the postcard rack where she'd been hiding and sidled on up to the front desk. "I've always wanted to go to the Columbia Icefields," Darlene said, "but I can't convince Dick to take me. The world's glaciers are receding, you know. They'll all be gone by the time I convince Dick to go see them!"

Alicia doubted that, but she did remember the vivid display of just how far the Athabasca Glacier had receded in the past ninety years. It was impressive.

Darlene sighed. "I just can't seem to pry my husband away from the fishing. Does your young man fish?"

Darlene was certainly fishing—for information—but Alicia refused to take the bait by either denying or confirming that Mitch was her young man. "He doesn't like to fish, no."

"You're lucky. Take my word for it. Don't get yourself hooked up with a fishing man—if you'll excuse the pun."

"I'll keep that in mind, Darlene. Meanwhile, here's a pamphlet on the Columbia Icefields that you can show your husband when he gets back. Otherwise, there are tours out of Jasper townsite that I'd be more than happy to sign you up for. You wouldn't have to go with your husband. You could always go on your own."

"I don't like tours. The people on them are so nosy. Oh, look, here come the Dennisons. Did you know they're bird watchers? They look so normal, too."

"They are normal!" Alicia retorted. The Dennisons, a young couple from Toronto, were particular favorites of hers. "And very nice."

"I didn't say they weren't nice. Just strange. All bird watchers are, you know. Hush now, here they come." Darlene turned to the Dennisons and said, "Hello, there. What have you two been up to?"

"We walked to the top of the Whistlers, looking for white-tailed ptarmigan," Meg Dennison replied. "It's one of several grouses of the genus *Lagopus,* having feathered feet. Rather rare. Imagine my relief at not having left my bins behind. I almost did, you know.''

"Yes, well..." Darlene backed up, looking at both the Dennisons as if they'd escaped from a funny farm. "I really must be going. So nice to chat with you."

The moment Darlene was gone, Alicia and the Dennisons looked at one another and cracked up.

"You lost me with the bins," Alicia confessed with a grin.

"Binoculars," Meg explained. "I know, I know. I shouldn't have gone on that way, but I couldn't help myself. That woman drives me up the wall sometimes! She treats us like we're—"

"Strange birds," Bill Dennison inserted.

"I've tried telling her that bird watching is one of the fastest growing sports in North America, but she won't listen to me," Alicia stated. "By the way, I wanted to say thanks for showing Nicole that gray jay. She's been keeping her eyes peeled for birds ever since."

"No thanks are necessary," Meg replied. "She seems like a nice little girl. Pretty, too."

"When she grows up, she's going to break somebody's heart," Bill quipped.

Alicia hoped not. She didn't want anyone's heart getting broken, including her own.

"Daddy, how do baby birds learn how to fly?"

They were on their way to the Columbia Icefields, and Nicole had been asking tough questions such as that since they'd left the lodge. Alicia gave Mitch a commiserating look and a shrug. It was his turn, she'd just struggled to explain why the sky was blue and not purple or polka-dot.

"How do baby birds learn how to fly?" Mitch repeated. "Very carefully, I'll bet." Alicia laughed, but Nicole showed no sign of appreciating his humor. He sighed and tried to sound knowledgeable. "The parent birds teach the young ones how to fly."

"Does the mommy teach them or does the daddy bird?" Nicole asked.

"Who do *you* think teaches them, Nicole?" Alicia returned, recognizing the panicked look on Mitch's face.

"I think the daddy bird does, when he's home," Nicole replied. "Otherwise, the mommy bird hires someone to do it."

Alicia's heart gave a funny little twinge. Nicole had given her quite a few of them since she'd come to visit. The first time had been when the little girl had solemnly informed Alicia that she was "too nice to be a mommy" and asked was that why she didn't have any kids of her own?

Then there had been the time Nicole had caught Alicia, who'd been chopping onions for Sloppy Joes for lunch, crying on the lodge's back porch. A smile lifted Alicia's lips as she recalled that one.

Nichole had come out of nowhere to sit beside her on the front step and put her hand on Alicia's shoulder. "Is it your time of month?" Nicole had solicitously asked.

Alicia had been so startled by the comment that she'd almost fallen off the steps.

"My mother says women always cry at their time of month," Nicole had stated matter-of-factly.

"She does, does she?"

"What time *is* the time of month? Daytime?"

"I'll tell you tomorrow," Alicia had said. *After I get a certain well-written book from the library that tells me how to answer delicate questions like that one!*

More recently, there had been the time they'd argued over Nicole's wearing a string bikini to the community pool. Mitch had asked Alicia to handle it. Nicole had pouted and hidden in her room, only to come out half an hour later— wearing a more appropriate swimsuit. She'd leaned her head on Alicia's shoulder and looked up at her with puppy-dog eyes. "Are you still my friend?"

What could she say? She'd nodded and given the little girl a giant hug.

The sound of Nicole's voice brought Alicia's thoughts back to the present.

"Daddy, how come snow is white and icicles aren't?"

"Isn't it your turn?" Mitch murmured in an aside to Alicia.

"She asked you," she whispered back.

"I give up, kiddo. How come snow is white and icicles aren't?"

Nicole gave a long-suffering sigh. "Dad-dy! I was asking you."

Alicia decided to give a harried Mitch a break. "That's an excellent question, Nicole. Tell you what. When we get back to the lodge, we'll look up the answer in a book my dad's got, okay?"

"I don't like books," Nicole stated. "I like TV."

"I read to her every night," Mitch said defensively.

"That's good," Alicia replied.

"Yeah, Daddy can sound just like Donald Duck."

"I had no idea that was one of your talents," Alicia murmured with a teasing look in his direction.

"Oh, I've got lots of talents you don't know about yet," he replied provocatively. "Just you wait."

"I will," she promised.

"Look, there are some animals! Can we stop and feed them?" Nicole pleaded. "They look hungry. They're even eating the dirt."

"We're not allowed to feed any animals in the national park," Alicia told Nicole. "Those are mountain goats, and they might get sick on people food."

"They'll get sick on dirt for sure," Nicole maintained.

"They get minerals from the dirt."

"Yuck. I bet they'd rather have a chocolate-chip cookie."

"No, they wouldn't."

"Grown-ups are mean."

"Nicole," Mitch said warningly.

"Well, they are. Making those poor animals eat dirt. And making me wear these dumb shoes."

"They're perfectly good walking shoes," Mitch maintained.

"I like my other shoes better. They have polka-dots."

"You might slip up on the ice if you wore your other shoes. You won't slip with these."

"Are we going ice skating?"

"No. I told you before. We're going to visit a glacier."

"Do they have pizza there?"

"No, they have ice there."

"Do we have to eat it?"

"No, we look at it."

"It sounds boring."

Mitch frowned. *Boring* had been his ex-wife's favorite word, and it irked him to see his daughter picking it up. "We're going to have fun," Mitch said, as if issuing an order.

Nicole sat back with another long-suffering sigh.

Despite the rather shaky beginning, they did, indeed, have fun once they reached the Columbia Icefields. Alicia was pleased to see that the good weather was holding up. Nicole was pleased to see the souvenir store next to the ticket counter.

"I love to shop," Nicole happily informed Alicia. "My mom even got me a book, when I was just a baby, about shopping. She likes it, too. She's an art buyer, you know."

"No, I didn't know."

"The best art buyer in the whole world!"

Yes, but was she the best mom in the whole world? As far as Alicia was concerned, that was the important question.

"So," Mitch said heartily, "everyone ready for our adventure?"

"What adventure?" Nicole asked him.

"The ride up to the glacier."

"I thought we were going to shop now," Nicole said.

"Later. Now we're going to go wait for the bus to pick us up."

Nicole left the store with a longing last look at a pair of seashell earrings that were nearly as tall as she was.

"Look, up there." Mitch pointed. "That's the Athabasca Glacier and that's where we're going."

"Why?" Nicole asked.

"Because it's there," Mitch stated, the way countless explorers had before him. "Put your sweatshirt on." He held it out for Nicole, who obligingly stuck her arms and head through the proper holes. "It's liable to be cold up there."

Not only was it cold, it was slippery as well, as Alicia discovered when she stepped out of the specially designed snowcoach that had taken them onto the glacier itself.

"Hang on to me," Mitch suggested, putting an arm around her waist.

She didn't need a second invitation. Her down vest was warm enough, but it felt as if her running shoes had ball bearings on the soles.

"If we're lucky, maybe we'll hear an avalanche," the guide said.

Alicia thought that was one kind of luck she could do without. For the time being, she just wanted to remain upright.

She soon regained her confidence once she'd stepped away from the snowcoach to a place where the footing was much better. "I'll be all right now," she assured Mitch. "You go on with Nicole. I want to take a picture or two."

"Or three dozen," he teased.

She checked the frame counter. "Unfortunately, I don't have that many left on the roll."

The trickling miniature stream of glacier water that had caught her attention wasn't far away. The light was hitting it just right, turning the runoff water a reflective aqua unique to glaciers. She bent down to get a better shot, leaning closer as she focused her lens. There. Her finger pressed the shutter button. That should get it.

Alicia straightened and was in the process of turning around when her feet suddenly started sliding out from under her. She panicked. Her camera, hanging on a strap around her neck, bounced against the front of her down vest as she windmilled her arms in a frantic attempt to stay upright.

A second later, Mitch was there, holding her with reassuring strength, steadying her on the slippery surface. His hands were warm on her waist. Her hands were on his chest, where she could feel the steady beat of his heart through his sweatshirt.

As they stood there gazing into each other's eyes, Alicia hazily thought that an avalanche could have occurred and she wouldn't have noticed. He was going to kiss her. She could feel it coming. Her lips parted. She watched his lips moving closer to hers and waited with baited breath for the brush of his mouth.

But it wasn't to be, as they were interrupted by the high-pitched sound of Nicole's voice. "What are you guys doing?"

They sprang apart so quickly, Alicia almost slipped again. "Careful," he murmured.

"We weren't doing anything, Nicole," Alicia said, feeling guilty without quite knowing why. "That is, I almost slipped and your dad helped me, that's all."

"Fibber," Mitch leaned down to whisper in her ear.

"Your face is all red," Nicole noted.

"It is?" Alicia raised her hands to her cheeks. "Must be sunburn. You can get sunburn real fast up here with the reflection on the snow and ice."

"I don't mind if you were hugging each other," Nicole nonchalantly assured them. "I know all about that stuff. I saw it on TV."

Knowing how unsupervised Nicole's TV viewing was, Alicia could imagine what the little girl had seen on TV!

Even Mitch appeared disconcerted. "Uh, we'll talk about that later. The bus is reloading. We'd better get back on board."

"I just want to know one thing. Does this mean I'm going to get a little brother or sister soon? I'd rather have a sister," Nicole informed an astonished Mitch and Alicia. "Boys are too sloppy."

"I thought she'd never go to sleep," Mitch said later that night after tucking Nicole in.

At Nicole's insistence, Alicia and Mitch had taken turns reading bedtime stories.

It was the first time Alicia had been inside the furnished cabin since Mitch had moved in. The "handyman's" cabin was the one directly behind the lodge, and the layout was the same as the lodge's other one-bedrooms with kitchenettes. She was curious to see how Mitch had put his own stamp on it.

She'd been a bit disappointed to find that his pickup truck held more clues to his personality than the cabin did. There were no personal touches here, no sign of it being a home, however temporary, except in the bedroom, which he'd given to Nicole while he slept on the hide-away bed in the living room.

Nicole's room did look lived in. The rest of the place looked as if he'd merely been passing time there. It was tidy, but austere.

"Thanks for staying," Mitch said. He sat down on the living room couch and patted the plaid seat cushion.

"No problem." Alicia accepted his silent invitation to sit beside him. "I couldn't resist Nicole's offer of a bedtime hug," she confessed with a grin. Nicole's hugs were never polite gestures. They were desperately heartfelt. She ate up attention faster than she did Gloria's cookies. "She had me hug each one of her dolls, too. How did she fit them all into her suitcase?"

"She didn't bring any of them with her." Iris always forgot to include any books or toys when she packed for Nicole. Mitch was used to that. "I bought her a few things when she got here."

"I saw that." He'd gotten her more than a few. "And I have to congratulate you on your Donald Duck impersonation." Hearing an Uncle Wiggley story read in a Donald Duck voice had been an experience, indeed. "It was very good."

"I know something else that's very good." He slowly pulled her into his arms. "This." His lips brushed hers, teasing her until she parted her lips.

Tasting her response, he intensified the kiss. He savored the warmth of her mouth, growling his pleasure as the tip of her tongue shyly touched his bottom lip. Before long, she was boldly greeting his tongue with her own, exploring the taste of him as he'd done with her.

The feel of Mitch's fingers on the buttons of her flannel shirt finally brought Alicia to her senses. Nicole was right in the other room. She could wake up at any moment and find them . . . flat out on the couch. How had they gotten that way? She frowned, trying to gather her scattered thoughts together. It wasn't easy to be coherent when Mitch was placing tempting kisses on her collarbone.

"Wait," she whispered. Clearing her throat, she tried again, this time with a little more backbone in it. "Wait!"

He lifted his head and stared down at her with blue eyes passionate enough to give her second thoughts. "What's wrong?"

"I can't do this." She resolutely freed herself from his arms. "Not with Nicole in the other room." She cast a nervous glance at the closed bedroom door.

"You're right. What we need is some time together—*alone*. Something romantic. What do you say?"

"Sounds promising."

"Oh, it will be. You can count on that." He sealed the pledge with a kiss.

Alicia stared at herself in the mirror. Mitch would be picking her up for their romantic dinner date any minute now. Gloria had volunteered for baby-sitting duty.

"You might not be gorgeous, but at least your dress is," she informed her reflection.

Made out of rayon in the same deep aqua as glacial water, the dress swirled around her legs every time she moved, making her feel deliciously feminine. The strappy sandals she wore with it heightened the effect—and added about two inches to her own height.

She wondered what Mitch would think of her outfit. What did he see when he looked at her? A woman or a companion for his daughter? Though she no longer believed he was trying to use her as an unpaid baby-sitter, sometimes she couldn't help worrying if part of her appeal might be the fact that she was good with Nicole.

But tonight wasn't the time for worrying or wondering. It was the time for enjoying. Too nervous to remain in her room, Alicia waited for Mitch on the lodge's stone porch. He arrived promptly and looked fabulous.

He'd traded his jeans and work shirt for a black suit and a stunning white dress shirt. Tucked under the shirt's collar was a black bolo tie with a traditional silver-and-turquoise setting. He'd left off his hat for once. And he'd brought her flowers.

"Carnations. My favorites. Thank you," she said.

"Hello there!" Darlene Humphries called out from the soda machine around the corner. "Are you two going somewhere?"

"Yes," Mitch replied, hurrying Alicia down the steps. "In fact, we're leaving now."

Their mad dash to Mitch's truck left Alicia breathless and laughing. "Quick, before she catches up with us," Mitch said, picking Alicia up as if she weighed no more than a feather and then quickly but carefully placing her in the passenger seat. The feel of his hands on her waist lingered long after he'd gotten in behind the steering wheel.

"We made it!" he announced with glee as they left the lodge behind.

"We certainly did. A brilliant getaway. Now where to?"

"You'll see."

She was delighted and a bit surprised at his choice—a four-star nouvelle-cuisine restaurant that had only recently opened outside of town.

"It has a lovely view of the mountains," he told her as they were seated.

How did he know that? she wondered. Had he brought another woman there before? She felt guilty for her jealous thoughts. Mitch wasn't hers. She had to keep reminding herself of that fact. They were just . . . friends? No. More than that. They were betwixt and between—caught in the never-never land between being friends and becoming lovers.

The idea of Mitch becoming her lover had Alicia reaching for a glass of ice water to cool down.

"You okay?" Mitch asked.

"Fine," she said from behind the shield of the menu. "Why do you ask?"

"You're holding your menu upside down."

"Oh." She quickly rectified the error. "That better?"

"It might make it easier to read. I'm having the steak," he announced. "How about you?"

Alicia couldn't resist smiling. The menu was filled with some tantalizingly unusual combinations—pork with plum sauce, duckling stuffed with cherries, halibut with citrus and pine nut butter sauce—yet he chose steak, in two seconds flat, no less. "I guess you're just a meat-and-potatoes sort of guy, eh?" she teased him, deciding on the slightly more exotic duckling herself.

"I believe in life's simple pleasures," he agreed, eyeing her as if she were one of those pleasures.

Alicia felt surprisingly nervous as she sat there, being wined and dined by him. Classical music played in the background, something soft and romantic. Debussy, she thought. Their window-side table faced the mountains with the rushing Athabasca River in the foreground.

Alicia felt as if she were caught in that river, caught up in the rapids of his attention, unable to direct her own course anymore. She'd gone white-water rafting once. It had been an exhilarating, frightening, exciting experience. Being with Mitch made her feel the same way.

She took another calming sip of ice water, noticing for the first time the ornate place mats outlining the history of the area.

"What have you found?" Mitch asked, looking at his own place mat. "I'll bet you already know all this stuff, right?"

Alicia nodded. "Part of my job at the lodge is answering guests' questions, giving them a little background information. Many of them are surprised to hear that Canada is the second largest country in the world." She shrugged. "I don't know, it must be the librarian in me, but I enjoy educating people about this special corner of the world, telling them some of the stories."

"I'll bet you're great at storytelling."

Alicia grinned. "Get me started and I'm hard to stop. There are some wonderful stories. Most people only want to hear the basics, though—like how Jasper got it's name."

"And the answer is?"

"The town was eventually named after the park and the park got its name from an early fur trapper whose first name was Jasper."

"Good thing his name wasn't Ebenezer or it might have been called Ebenezer National Park."

She laughed. "Somehow I have a feeling they would have kept searching for another name instead of settling for that one."

"What about you? Why are you still searching instead of settling down?"

His question caught her by surprise. "Who says I'm searching?" she parried.

"We're all searching in one way or another."

"For what?" she asked.

"Happiness."

"I am happy. Very," she said softly, looking at him in a way meant to let him know he was one of the reasons for her happiness. "How about you?"

"The same."

"There you go again," she teased him, "overwhelming me with your enthusiasm."

"So, you want to be overwhelmed?" he returned with a devilish smile. "Wait until after dinner and I'll be more than glad to overwhelm you. In the dark, where only the stars can see us."

She had no doubt he'd be able to overwhelm her. The question was, would *she* ever be able to overwhelm *him?*

Later that evening, he did kiss her, in the dark, with only the stars, just as he'd promised; and he seemed to be as breathless as she was. As bothered and almost as overwhelmed. She was delighted.

They were in the front seat of his pickup, parked in a deserted parking lot up by the Whistlers, the mountain above Jasper.

"I've never made out in the front seat of a pickup before," she confessed in between kisses.

"No?"

"No." *But I plan on giving it my best effort,* she decided with that recklessness he always seemed to bring out in her.

"How are you enjoying it so far?" he asked in a seductive whisper.

"Mmm."

Words were forgotten as his kiss deepened, drawing her into its magic. She held nothing back. She loved kissing him, being kissed by him, and she let him know it.

Tremors of excitement shivered up her spine as his tongue boldly demanded more of her. She responded with eager abandon, following his fiery lead. Her lips moved over his with matching hunger, her tongue welcoming the touch of his. He made her feel wicked, powerful and very vulnerable.

"Lisha. You're a witch," he murmured as he kissed the line of her throat. "What you do to me..."

"What do I do to you?" she whispered as if she couldn't feel the strength of his arousal against her.

"Drive me crazy."

She couldn't think anymore, could hardly even breathe. But she didn't care. She could do those things later. For now, she wanted to keep the magic going. She'd never felt this way before.

She made no protest when his tongue slipped between her lips to once again woo and seduce her. She welcomed him, sighing her pleasure.

Time quickly lost its meaning. Alicia vaguely realized she was sprawled across his lap, but had no recollection of moving there. It was where she wanted to be. This way she could slide her arms around his waist and hold him. She could slip her fingers beneath the buttons of his shirt and feel the warmth of his skin, the thunder of his heart.

Her breathing became ragged as he caressed her breast with loving hands. He brushed his fingers against the ultra-sensitive peak, the soft material of her dress amplifying each suggestive stroke. His touch was exhilaratingly persuasive.

Alicia arched against him, her head tipped back. A split second later she saw stars. Only this time Mitch wasn't responsible.

"Ouch!" Both of Alicia's hands flew from his shoulders to rub the back of her head, which had just made contact with something solid. She groaned.

"What happened?" he asked.

"I think I just got some sense knocked into me by your truck's steering wheel," she noted unsteadily, blinking the tears from her eyes.

He gently pulled her back into his arms. "Show me where it hurts," he crooned. "I'll kiss it better."

"Oh, no, you don't." She placed her hand on his chest. "That's how I got knocked senseless in the first place."

"I thought my kisses did that."

"Very funny." Alicia reached around to feel the back of her head. "I think I'm getting a goose egg." She sighed. "I should have known better than to fool around in the front seat of a truck.'' Other people did that. Not practical Alicia.

''I agree. We're both old enough to know better. Didn't seem to stop either one of us, though, did it?''

''What do you think that means?''

''That we've got it bad. The question is, what are we going to do about it?''

''And the answer is . . . ?'' she asked.

''I'll tell you one thing.'' He reluctantly set her back in the passenger seat. ''Next time we definitely choose a better place for fooling around!''

Seven

Alicia was kneeling on a gardening pad, weeding the flower patch on the south side of the lodge, when a pair of little hands covered her eyes. "Guess who?"

"Minnie Mouse?"

"No."

"Pippi Longstocking?" Alicia had been reading the book to Nicole and it had become one of the little girl's favorites.

"That's right!" Nicole giggled and removed her hands. "I'm Pippi Longstocking!"

"Funny. You look like Nicole to me," Mitch said from behind them.

"Dad-dy!" The little girl's voice was filled with exasperation. "We were just playing around."

"Oh. I see. Playing around, eh?" Mitch looked at Alicia, letting her know that he wouldn't mind indulging in a few games with her himself. "Sounds like fun."

"Yes, it does," Alicia agreed with a demure smile.

"Here comes Red," Nicole said. The Irish setter dropped the Frisbee with a hopeful look in their direction. A moment later Nicole and Red bounded off together amid a cacophony of barks and girlish giggles.

"I want to play, too," Mitch murmured, kissing the side of Alicia's neck, which had been left bare by her ponytail.

She shivered. "I know."

"It's been almost two weeks."

"Mmm." She tilted her head the other way so he could kiss that side, as well. "I know."

Alicia was as aware of the passage of time since that steamy session in his pickup truck as he was. They had yet to find a suitable place for more than a few long, slow kisses and some all-too-brief embraces. There was always Mitch's cabin, but Alicia never knew when Nicole was going to pop out of the bedroom, demanding a glass of water or another bedtime story. She couldn't relax there.

"You'd think we could find someplace to be alone in this huge national park," he muttered.

"We tried. Remember?"

His groan ruffled the tendrils of hair curling at the nape of her neck. "I remember, all right. How did Pyramid Lake get that crowded?"

"It's the height of the tourist season. Which means there are people everywhere, unless you go backpacking into the wilderness—where there are always the bears to contend with. It's not as if we haven't tried. The fates just seem to be conspiring against us," she noted.

"It does feel that way, doesn't it?"

"It feels...wonderful." She captured his wandering hand. "But we'd better stop this before someone sees us."

He released her with obvious reluctance. "There are entirely too many someones around here," he growled.

"Good thing, too, or we'd all be out of a job. Did my dad tell you the lodge is booked solid through late August?"

Mitch groaned. "Yeah, he told me."

"Look on the bright side. At least Darlene Humphries has gone home."

"Thank heaven for small favors. But she was replaced by the Thompson triplets."

"Are they the ones who flushed their bottle down the toilet?"

"They sure are. It took me all day yesterday and most of this morning to fix it."

"We have been having more than our fair share of maintenance problems lately, haven't we? What with all the jammed windows and that broken oil heater, I haven't had a chance to invite you to Julie's picnic. It's this coming Saturday."

"I have to work Saturday."

"I know your boss. I'm sure I can finagle a well-deserved day off for you," she stated with an impish grin. "I thought we could bring Nicole, as well. There will be lots of kids there. What do you say?"

"Okay."

"Your enthusiasm overwhelms—"

He kissed her until she was breathless. Setting his hat back on his head, he said, "You were saying?"

"Nothing," she gasped with a bemused smile. "Nothing at all."

"Good."

"I thought you said this picnic was just for a few of Julie's friends," Mitch said. "Judging by the number of parked cars, it looks like half of Jasper townsite is here."

"I said friends and family," Alicia replied. "Julie's got lots of both."

"My hair's ugly," Nicole moaned.

"It looks fine," Mitch reassured her.

Alicia admitted she was no pro when it came to using a curling iron on a little girl's hair, but she thought she'd done a pretty good job—all things considered. Unfortunately, Nicole didn't agree. She'd been in that kind of mood all day.

"I hate my dress!" Nicole announced.

"I hate mine, too," Alicia said, although the blue chambray jumper was actually a favorite of hers. The white T-shirt she wore under it was cool and comfortable, key requirements for one of Julie's picnics. She'd learned, however, that the fastest way to end Nicole's complaints was to agree with them. "Let's go have fun anyway. Come on."

She took one of Nicole's hands and Mitch took the other. As they walked across the street together, Alicia felt a familiar warmth creeping into her heart. The bonds were growing stronger. So was the sense of belonging—she with them and they with her. It was too late to pull back now.

"Lift," Mitch announced as they neared the curb.

Alicia obligingly lifted her half of Nicole until the little girl was dangling in the air for the step or two it took for them to walk over the curb. Nicole forgot all about hating her hair and her dress as she giggled at this favorite maneuver of hers.

"Again," she shouted. "Do it again!"

They did, to the accompaniment of more girlish giggles.

Mitch and his daughter both hesitated once they reached the backyard and realized how large the gathering really was.

Alicia tugged on Nicole's hand, bringing Mitch along, as well. "Come on, you two slowpokes," she drawled, snitching one of Mitch's favorite expressions. "I'll introduce you around."

After the first five minutes, Mitch knew he'd never remember everyone's name, so he gave up trying. But they were all good people, he could tell that much. And they knew how to party.

There was plenty of food and plenty of entertainment in the form of everything from basketball to horseshoes. To his surprise, Nicole quickly joined in with the other kids, deserting him and Alicia.

"She'll be fine," Alicia assured him, reading his worried look. "Geoffrey is Julie's oldest and he'll look after Nicole. You should see how good he is with his little sister."

Mitch didn't look very convinced.

"How are you going to cope when Nicole starts dating?" she teased him.

"She's not allowed to do that until she's thirty!" he declared with a hint of paternal desperation.

"Here, you look like you could use a cold beer." Alicia handed him a can from the metal washtub filled with ice. "Now, about Nicole's dating . . ."

Mitch groaned.

They caught up with Nicole again while standing in line for food. The selection included cold cuts as well as hot dogs and hamburgers straight off the grill. "My daddy lets me have hot dogs and potato chips for dinner all the time," Nicole was bragging to the child in front of her.

"He doesn't make you eat broccoli?"

Nicole shook her head. "Never."

"Lucky you," the child stated enviously. "I wish *my* folks were like that!"

The children moved ahead, while Alicia eyed Mitch disapprovingly. "You call that dinner? Do you know what's in hot dogs?"

"No—" he piled two on his paper plate "—and I don't want to know. Nicole loves them."

Alicia speared several cubes of ham and cheese with a toothpick. "I'm sure she loves ice cream, too, but you wouldn't let her eat that all the time, would you?"

"No?"

"No."

"Isn't ice cream one of the five basic food groups?" Mitch countered.

"There are four food groups, not five. Have you really been giving her nothing but junk food all summer long?"

"Define junk food."

Alicia rolled her eyes.

"I was just kidding," Mitch assured her. "Of course I haven't been feeding my daughter nothing but hot dogs all summer."

"That's a relief."

"Sometimes we have macaroni-and-cheese or hamburgers. In Denver, Nicole eats sushi. Can you believe it?" He shuddered. "No wonder she longs for a good burger."

Alicia knew it was bound to happen, sooner or later the men would all congregate on one side of the lawn, leaving the women behind. Some things never changed.

"Great party," Alicia told Julie. "What are you doing?" this as Julie dragged her off to the kitchen.

"You're in love with Mitch!" Julie stated.

Alicia blinked. "What?"

"I saw the way you were looking at him, and if that's not love, I'll eat my sneakers."

"You're crazy, do you know that?"

"And you're crazy, too. About him."

"I think you've been out in the sun too long." Alicia put a teasing hand on her friend's forehead. "Maybe you should go upstairs. Rest. You'll feel better tomorrow."

"Actually, I won't feel better tomorrow," Julie replied. "I'm pregnant. Which means I'll be as nauseated tomorrow morning as I was this morning."

"Really? That's great news! Congratulations!" Alicia hugged her. "Shouldn't you be sitting down or something?"

"I'm fine. You're the one I'm worried about."

"Me? What on earth for?"

"Because you're falling in love with a guy who's a rolling stone at best and a drifter at worst. Either way, you'll be going back to Minneapolis in a few weeks and he'll be going heaven knows where. Or has that slipped your mind?"

"Of course it hasn't slipped my mind," Alicia said. "And Mitch isn't a drifter. He's very responsible. I think he may be ready to put down roots— Stop giving me that look."

"What look?"

"The same look you gave me when I wanted to dye my hair blond. That doubtful look."

"I was right to be doubtful."

"I care for Mitch, and I think he cares for me."

Julie immediately pounced on that. "You only *think* he cares?"

"Gee, if I'd have known I was going to face this kind of inquisition, I would have had him fill out a ten-page form listing his intentions," Alicia retorted. "Lighten up, would you please?"

"I just don't want to see you get hurt again."

"I'm not real eager to repeat the experience myself," Alicia noted. "But I'm not about to let what happened to me in the past deprive me of having a future."

"A future with Mitch?"

"Maybe. That depends."

"On what?"

"On whether or not you ever let me out of this kitchen!" Alicia retorted. "Stop worrying about me. Worry about taking good care of yourself and little junior in there. I can take care of myself."

"Famous last words," Julie muttered.

"So, Mitch, how do you like it here in Jasper?" Julie's husband, David, asked him.

"I like it fine."

"Plan on staying long?"

"Haven't decided yet."

"Thought about settling down?"

"Thought about it."

"Not ready yet, eh?"

"I wouldn't say that."

David gave him a man-to-man stare, which Mitch met without flinching. Finally, as if satisfied with what he saw, David nodded and handed Mitch another beer. "I hear you like hockey. How about those Flames?"

"Are you ever going to let me out of this kitchen?" Alicia inquired while chewing on a carrot stick.

"I'm pregnant. Humor me."

"Okay, but only for five more minutes, max."

"Tell me what you see in the guy."

Alicia raised her eyebrows.

"Other than the obvious," Julie clarified. "When you first met him, you told me that he wasn't your type. Something about him being too rugged, too sure of himself..."

"That was before I really got to know him. Did I tell you that he thinks I'm hell on wheels? He even called me a blood-thirsty little devil the first time we met."

"How romantic of him."

"Don't you understand? He sees a part of me that no one else does. To him, I'm not always practical or sensible. With him, I can be reckless sometimes."

"If you're planning on being reckless, I hope you'll take proper precautions. Here—" Julie opened a top kitchen cabinet and reached behind several bottles of vitamins "—you better take these." She handed Alicia a tastefully decorated box of...condoms.

Startled, Alicia handed them right back to her.

"Would you rather buy some in town?" Julie inquired.

"No! I've known Mr. Drummond, the pharmacist, since I was eight."

"That's what I figured." She gave the box to Alicia again. "Put them in your purse. Just in case."

"You're impossible!"

"You're welcome."

"You keep them in the kitchen cabinet?" Alicia asked even as she hurriedly stuffed the box in her purse.

"Obviously we haven't been using them much lately," Julie replied, patting her tummy. "Besides, it's a safe hiding place. The kids avoid this cabinet like the plague. I keep the prune juice in there!"

"Looking for Alicia?" David asked, noticing Mitch's wavering attention. "She's probably in the kitchen with my wife. Julie's got some news she wanted to tell her. I might as well tell you, as well, you'll hear it from Alicia soon enough. Julie's pregnant again."

"Congratulations."

"Thanks. But I still haven't figured out how to raise the first two yet."

"Yeah, I know what you mean."

"They never slow down. I've clocked them. They can go three, four hours without stopping, unless they run into each other."

"Too bad we can't harness that energy," Mitch said.

"In the old days it was easy. All we had to do as fathers was bring home the paycheck, hit them when they were bad, play a few games of basketball with them when they were good. That's all my dad ever did. But now we do everything from change diapers to holding them when they get sick. But you know something? I feel closer to my kids than I think my dad ever felt to me. And that's something I wouldn't trade for anything."

It had been a long time since Mitch had thought back to the days when he'd helped change Nicole's diapers. Frankly, at the time, it hadn't always seemed that wonderful an experience. Smelly and messy, yes.

But looking back, he remembered how sweet Nicole would smell after her bath, or how she'd smile at him despite the fact that Iris had claimed she was too young to smile yet. In those days, he'd gotten excited about the perfection of her tiny little fingers and toes, about her first step and her first word. Where had the time gone?

He looked at her now and saw a little girl on the verge of . . . throwing a cupcake.

"Nicole, put that down this second!"

"Ah, fatherhood. Ain't it grand?" David murmured with a grin.

"Looks like the crowd's thinning out a bit," Julie noted as she and Alicia returned outside.

"I thought I heard Mitch yelling a minute ago. Do you see him?" Alicia asked.

"He's talking to David. Looks calm to me."

"And Nicole?"

"She's over there eating cupcakes with Geoffrey and the rest of the kids."

"Oh-oh," Alicia said, noticing the adoring look Nicole was giving Geoffrey. "I think we've got a case of puppy love here."

"Think you'll survive parenthood?" David asked Mitch.

"I don't know how you cope with two."

"I've got help. Damn, this washtub is leaking," David exclaimed, setting down his beer and rescuing the remaining cans. "I better pour this ice out of here before the entire table floods. Mitch, there's an extra washtub in the shed at the back of the lot. Would you mind getting it for me?"

"No problem," Mitch said, already on his way.

When he opened the door to the metal shed, he could see the washtub from where he stood, but he had to step inside to reach it. The next thing he knew, the door had slammed behind him, shutting out the sun. He was thrown into total darkness.

The panic hit Mitch with the force of a landslide. One minute he was fine, the next he was fighting off the demons. He was trapped...trapped beneath tons of rubble. His men were counting on him, depending on him to get them out. He had to think straight, had to conserve oxygen.

His leg, he couldn't feel his leg! He heard the moans through the inky darkness. His mind went as numb as his leg.

He tried to claw his way out. His voice was frozen in his throat as the last of the oxygen trickled away.

"Mitch, are you all right in there?" Alicia called out. There was no answer.

Concerned, she opened the door to the shed and found Mitch standing inside, blinking at the sunlight. His face was ashen, his hands shaking. "What is it?"

The door slammed behind her as she rushed toward him. "Damn, Julie's husband's been meaning to fix this stupid door. Just a second, I can't see a thing in here." Alicia felt along the metal for the tricky clasp that opened the door. Then she propped it ajar with a brick. "There. Now tell me what happened?"

Mitch shook his head, trying to clear the images from his mind. They weren't real, he kept telling himself. He was safe now. They were just dreams, memories, nightmares. But the sweat on his forehead and the shakiness of his limbs felt very real.

"Mitch...?"

"Nothing," he said hoarsely. "It's nothing."

"Don't give me that. I can tell something's wrong."

He brushed past her into the sunlight, taking huge gulps of fresh air as if he hadn't breathed any in a year.

"Do you have claustrophobia?" she gently asked him. "Is that it? It's nothing to be embarrassed about. We've all got phobias. Get me on a tall escalator and I'm a basket case."

Mitch knew he was a basket case, all right. Even after he'd gotten out of the hospital, he hadn't been able to go near a construction site. He got the shakes so bad that he almost fell flat on his face. He was useless, just as he'd been useless to help those two men who'd died in the building collapse.

Sure, they all told him it wasn't his fault, but he'd seen the look on his crew's faces when they'd seen him shaking. *Poor guy, he's gone over the edge. Just like he did in that collapse. Two good men dead. Damn shame.* He'd heard that a lot. *Damn shame.*

The shame had been deep inside him, eating away at his soul. To this day, Mitch couldn't remember which had come first—the collapse of the building or the collapse of his marriage to Iris. In his mind, the two happened simultaneously. He'd left Denver before the ink on the divorce papers was dry, before he'd recovered completely from his injuries. As if he could ever really recover. The doctors told him there was no permanent damage. None that they could find. The real damage was inside him.

Coming to the mountains had been a godsend. He'd worked his way north from Colorado to Montana, then Wyoming, until crossing into Canada. New country. New life. The farther away from Denver he'd gotten, the better he'd felt. He loved the feeling of blue sky over his head, the simple life of working with his hands again, dealing with the small problems one man could solve instead of trying to change the skyline of a city.

The nightmares had lessened, allowing him to sleep through the night for the first time in months. Now they filled his head again.

Alicia recognized that look in his eyes, although she'd never seen it so nakedly displayed before. The regret, the suffering was there. She wanted to put her arms around him, tell him it would be all right. But the stiff set of his shoulders told her that any gestures of comfort wouldn't be appreciated right now.

"Come on." She took his hand in hers. "Let's go for a walk."

"Nicole..."

"Will be fine with Julie. She'll look after her. Besides, Nicole is fascinated with Julie's son, Geoffrey. I think she's got a crush on him."

Mitch didn't say a word, confirming her suspicion that something was terribly wrong. Mitch's hand was cold and clammy in hers. She twined her fingers through his and held on tight, willing him to come back to her from whatever nightmarish hole he was in. "Come on. Let's go."

They walked for several blocks, not saying anything. She could feel him gradually relaxing. The warmth came back to his hand, and his breathing sounded less ragged.

"Want to tell me what went on back there?" she quietly asked him.

"It's pretty obvious. I don't care for cramped spaces."

"I got that impression. Do you know why?"

"Yeah," he said bitterly. "I know why."

"Care to tell me?"

"No."

The door slammed in her face with just that one word. No. End of discussion. Do Not Enter. Dead End.

It hurt. She thought they'd progressed beyond that. It was a standoff. He didn't want to tell her, and she didn't want to press him. But she did wish that he'd share his feelings, including his fears, with her. It would be a sign that he cared about her.

It didn't help matters any that later that same evening, Alicia walked into Mitch's living room to find Nicole with a pair of scissors in her hand and shorn strands of her dark hair on the floor. Nicole had cut it as close to her head as possible, except for one long strand down the middle of her back that she'd obviously been unable to reach.

"Nicole!" Alicia hurriedly grabbed the scissors away from her. "What are you doing?"

"Cutting my hair."

"But why?"

"I want Geoffrey to like me. He said girls were dumb, always fixing their hair and stuff and that he only wanted to be with boys. I figured that if I looked more like a boy, he'd like me better."

"Oh, Nicole ... What's your father going to say?"

"My God!" Mitch exclaimed from the cabin's doorway. He turned to glare at Alicia. "What the hell did you do to her?"

Alicia resented his implication. Her back stiffened as she indignantly protested, "*I* didn't do anything! Nicole did it all by herself."

"I don't believe this. Why on earth would you chop your hair off, Nicole?" Mitch asked in bewilderment. "Is this some new kind of fashion statement?"

"It's a secret," Nicole replied with a warning look at Alicia.

Mitch exploded. "What do you mean, 'it's a secret'? I asked you a question, young lady, and I expect an answer! I'm taking Red for a walk, and you'd better have a reasonable explanation for your actions by the time I come back. God knows what your mother's going to say when she sees you.''

Alicia wondered which worried him more—Nicole's actions or his ex-wife's reaction to Nicole's new look.

"I think you should tell your father what you told me," Alicia advised Nicole once they were along again in the cabin.

"I can't talk to him about—" Nicole looked around and lowered her voice to a bare whisper "—boys!"

"Sure you can."

"That's woman stuff! He wouldn't understand."

"What if I tell him?" Alicia suggested.

"No!"

She tried another tack. "Nicole, your dad was a boy once himself. Maybe he can give you some tips about Geoffrey."

"You think so?" Nicole looked doubtful.

"Maybe. But a word of advice. If a boy doesn't like you just the way you are, don't cut your hair off to please him."

"Should I have punched him?" Nicole asked.

"Good heavens, no! What gave you that idea?"

"Geoffrey seems to like to get punched. His other friends do it to him all the time."

"Just be yourself. And if he doesn't like you, that's his problem."

"And *that's* when you punch him."

"No. Punching is out." Tempting as it may be on occasion, Alicia silently tacked on. "I really think that you should tell your father the truth about why you cut your hair."

"You're not my mother. You can't tell me what to do," Nicole muttered.

The words struck Alicia like a stake through the heart. She hadn't seen them coming. She'd heard the defiant phrase enough times from students at work. Logically, she knew how to respond. Her emotional response was another matter entirely. She felt black-and-blue inside. "I may not be your mother," she said quietly, "but I still say you should tell your father the truth."

"You can't make me!" Nicole shouted before going into her room and slamming the door.

Alicia promised herself she wasn't going to cry. Sure it had been a traumatic day, but that was no reason to turn on the waterworks. She'd be calm and strong—a veritable oak tree of dependability. But first she needed a Kleenex.

Knowing Mitch kept a box hidden in the end-table drawer, away from Nicole's compulsive consumption, she looked there. She found more than she was looking for.

The picture frame was silver and the face looking up at her was fashion-model beautiful. Across the bottom in perfect script were written the words "To Nicole. Love, Mommy."

Iris was obviously not the effusive type. But she must have been Mitch's type at one time. Otherwise, why would he have made her his wife? And if this was his type of woman, Alicia didn't have a prayer.

Alicia stared down at the picture, looking for some flaw, some indication that the photograph had been touched up. Nothing but perfection stared back at her. She sat there transfixed, like someone staring into the eyes of a snake—unable to look away.

The sound of Red's bark alerted her to Mitch's return. She considered putting the photograph back where she'd found it, but she'd had enough prevarication. She stayed as she was.

"Where's Nicole?" Mitch demanded.

"In her room. Why didn't you tell me your ex-wife was gorgeous?" Alicia asked, lifting her eyes to meet Mitch's. She wanted to see his reaction. She wanted to understand. But his eyes gave nothing away except impatience.

"I didn't tell you because it's irrelevant."

"How can you be attracted to me when you were married to her? There's no way I could ever be like her—" Alicia ran her fingers over the perfect cheekbones "—not unless I got plastic surgery."

"I don't want you to be like her." Mitch forcefully grabbed the photograph away from her, tossed it back into the drawer and slammed it shut. "She put me through hell! Do you think I'd want to repeat that? I may have been taken in by a pretty face once, but that's a mistake I'll never make again!"

Ah, a pretty face. Alicia knew she certainly wasn't that. And it wasn't much consolation to hear Mitch stating that he'd never be taken in again. Given that attitude, it made sense that he'd go for someone plain and ordinary like herself. Probably *anybody* plain and ordinary and good with kids would do. That meant he still wasn't seeing her, Alicia, as someone special, someone different.

"Is that why you're attracted to me?" she demanded, determined to face her fears head-on. "Because I'm so unlike your ex-wife?"

"No. Why is it so hard for you to accept that I'm attracted to you because of you?"

"I'd believe it more if you'd have been upfront with me about everything from the beginning—about your ex-wife and about Nicole."

"So we're back to that, are we?"

"It appears we are. If I'm unsure of you, it's because you keep things from me. The situation at the picnic this afternoon was a perfect example. You shut me out."

"There are some things I can't talk about," he stated flatly.

"There are a *lot* of things you can't talk about. You always leave me guessing in the dark."

"What's there to guess about? Why do you have to know every damn thing about me?"

"I don't have to know every damn thing," she retorted, "but a few basics would be nice."

"You do know the basics. You know all you need to know."

"I know all you *want* me to know. There's a difference."

"Not to me there isn't. The bottom line here is that I care about you, but you're too stubborn to believe me. Instead, you go looking for trouble around every corner."

"I don't go looking for trouble, but I agree with you, it does seem to jump out at me from around every corner. And it's because you won't talk to me, confide in me."

"No it's not. It's because you imagine problems where there are none."

"Are you trying to tell me that I imagined how upset you were this afternoon when you were locked in that tool shed?"

Mitch bristled at being reminded of his momentary weakness. "Did it ever occur to you that if you didn't push so hard, I might be more tempted to tell you?"

"I haven't pushed hard. If you think I have, I apologize," she said stiffly.

He sighed. "Now you're getting all uppity on me."

"You don't like uppity? Fine. How's this for blunt and down-to-earth—you can keep your damn secrets to yourself as far as I'm concerned!" Alicia shouted before storming out of his cabin.

Eight

Midnight. The witching hour. Alicia couldn't sleep. It was Mitch's fault. He'd given her entirely too many restless nights, she decided with annoyance. He was the reason she was sitting here at the lodge's kitchen table in the middle of the night, sipping milk and nibbling on a banana-walnut muffin.

The sound of footsteps in the hallway startled her. "Dad! What are you doing up this late?"

"Couldn't sleep," he mumbled. "Gloria was keeping me awake. She was thinking too loudly."

Alicia was sure she couldn't have heard him correctly. "She was what?"

"Thinking too loudly. She was lying there, and I could practically hear the wheels turning in her head."

"You're kidding, right?"

"He's not kidding," Gloria replied as she joined them at the large pine table. "Pass one of those muffins this way.

Thanks. Anyway, I was just lying there, minding my own business—"

"*Minding* being the operative word here," Ray inserted.

"When out of the blue, or out of the dark actually, your father asks me what I'm thinking about."

"A valid question," Ray maintained.

"And tells me that I'm keeping him awake."

"Her mind was going a mile a minute."

"I wasn't moving a muscle," Gloria protested.

"We've been married twenty-two years. I can tell when you're thinking too hard," Ray stated.

"He told me to stop it and go to sleep. I tried. Ten minutes later, he tells me that if I don't stop thinking so loud he's going to go sleep on the couch."

"I came in the kitchen instead," Ray said.

"For my muffins," Gloria noted.

As Alicia sat there, listening to their loving grumbling, she thought to herself, *This is what I want. To sit across the table from someone who knows me better than I know myself sometimes. Someone who cares enough to hear my unspoken thoughts. Someone who'll care enough to still be there twenty-two years later.*

Was Mitch capable of giving her what she wanted? Would he ever care for her the way she cared for him? Or was he just searching for someone who was the antithesis of his ex-wife? Excusing herself, she left the kitchen, still searching for answers.

Alicia sat curled up on her bedroom window seat, her fingers absently smoothing the faded pink material of the pillow she was hugging. She could see Mitch's cabin window from here. His light was still on. Was he brooding the same way she was?

Before meeting Mitch, she'd never considered herself to be the brooding type. But Mitch had changed the way she perceived herself in several areas. On the one hand, he'd opened up a reckless side she hadn't explored in years. On the other, he also opened up some self-doubts that were painful for her to deal with.

Alicia had no illusions about herself. She could accept who she was. She just wasn't sure Mitch could or would. And stumbling over these unexpected secrets of his only made it worse. He kept things from her. She knew sharing was difficult for him, but these surprises were becoming hard for her to cope with.

If only she knew where she stood with him. If only she knew how he really felt about her. If only he could love her...

Alicia spent the next day in a fog, the result of having spent most of the night sitting in her window seat. She only saw Mitch from a distance, and she didn't see Nicole at all.

Perhaps it was just as well. Alicia needed some time to reevaluate things. But she missed them. Which was silly, since neither Mitch nor Nicole had actually gone anywhere. It merely felt like they had.

Alicia didn't want to talk to anyone, which made dealing with guests a little difficult. In the end, she decided she was probably doing more harm than good by sticking around, so she asked Gloria to take over for her and went for a walk down by the river.

That's where Julie found her later that afternoon. "You left this at the picnic yesterday." Julie handed Alicia her watch. "It must have fallen off your wrist when we were in the kitchen. I thought you might miss it."

"Not half as much as I miss Mitch," Alicia murmured.

"Trouble in paradise?"

"You could say that. You may have been right to warn me about Mitch yesterday."

"Maybe. Then again, I may have been full of hot air."

Alicia looked at her in surprise. "What's this? You're changing your mind?"

"I'm leaving it open. Why don't you tell me what happened to change yours?"

"His ex-wife is gorgeous."

"Yes." Julie looked at her expectantly. "And . . . ?"

"And I'm not."

"So?"

"So why would a man who married an incredibly beautiful woman like that be interested in me?"

"I could give you half a dozen reasons."

"Too bad Mitch couldn't."

"Did you give him a chance to?"

"We had an argument," Alicia admitted.

"About his ex-wife being beautiful."

Put that way, it sounded rather silly. "No. We argued about the fact that he won't confide in me."

"I don't know Mitch well at all," Julie admitted, "but he doesn't seem like the kind of man who confides easily. You haven't known him that long, Alicia. Maybe it takes a while for him to share things."

"He said I pushed him too hard."

"And that hurt, didn't it?"

"Damn right it did." Alicia bit her lip and looked out over the rushing water. "How do things get so complicated?"

"Beats me. They say the road to true love is never straight."

"You've got that right. It's more like this river. Filled with unexpected turns and tricky rapids. Not easy to negotiate."

"But negotiating is crucial in order for love to survive."

"Is that the secret?"

"Let's just say it's a necessary ingredient."

"So you're telling me that I shouldn't push Mitch so hard. That I should let him have his secrets and wait until he decides to tell me."

"I suggested negotiation," Julie stated dryly, "not unconditional surrender. Talk to him, tell him how you feel. Then listen to him. See if there isn't some way you can clear this up."

"Yesterday you were warning me off Mitch, reminding me he's a drifter...."

"I'm pregnant. I'm entitled to mood changes every now and again. Besides, at first I was too busy noticing the way you were looking at Mitch to bother watching the way *he* was looking at *you*. David noticed it. I did, too, when I calmed down."

"And how does Mitch look at me?"

"Like you're his only hope for peace in a world gone crazy. Like you delight and amaze him."

Alicia was shaken. "You got all that from a look?"

"What can I say? I'm extraordinarily perceptive."

"Or overly imaginative."

"Why shouldn't he look at you that way? Don't you think you're worthy of having a man look at you like that?"

"It's not a matter of being worthy or not. It's a matter of believing."

"I can't help you there. You're on your own, kid."

"Gee, thanks."

"What did you expect? A magic wand?"

"That would be nice."

"You know, when I first met David, you gave me some pretty good advice."

"I did?"

Julie nodded. "You said to trust my heart, but not to ignore my head. Then you added the clincher."

"Which was?"

"It takes two to tango...." Julie began.

"And it takes two to argue," Alicia completed.

"Bingo."

By the time twilight rolled around, Alicia knew what she was going to do. She was going to talk to Mitch. She was going to speak her mind and most importantly, she was going to stay calm and listen to him.

He cared about her, a nugget of information she'd almost overlooked in the heat of their argument. It gave her the strength to overcome her nervousness and head over to Mitch's cabin.

Alicia had her hand raised to knock on the front door when she heard the sound of voices through the open window.

"Alicia doesn't like me anymore," Nicole stated flatly.

"That's not true," Mitch assured her. "She thinks you're great. So do I."

"Then why were you two fighting?"

"That's a hard question to answer, kiddo. But it didn't have anything to do with you. It wasn't your fault. When you grow up and have a family, then you'll understand that sometimes an argument isn't anyone's fault."

"I don't want a family," Nicole aloofly informed him.

"Why wouldn't you want a family?"

"Because kids just get in the way. They just cause problems."

"Oh, kiddo..."

Alicia heard Mitch's voice crack and felt the tears rush to her eyes.

"Come here, you." Even from this distance, Alicia could detect the fierce emotion in his voice. "I love you, kiddo. You have *never* been in the way. Never! You've brought me joy from the moment you were born, and you still bring me joy. Being your father, watching you grow up into such a sweet, smart young lady has been the best thing, the most

rewarding thing I've ever done in my entire life. Now sometimes parents are dumb and don't tell you things, like how
we feel. But that's our fault, not yours. Never doubt that I
love you. And if I don't tell you that often enough, just kick
me to remind me. Okay?''

"Okay. I love you, too, Daddy."

Half-blinded by tears, Alicia turned away. Wanting to
give father and daughter some quiet time together, she tip-
toed off the porch. She didn't go far, just to the back porch
of the lodge. From there she could keep an eye on Mitch's
cabin.

She hugged her arms around her knees as she sat there,
loving Mitch so much that it hurt. At some point, Red ma-
terialized out of the darkness to join her.

"I love him, Red," she whispered. "He's a fine man. The
best."

Red nodded her agreement.

Since Mitch hadn't closed the drapes, she could see him
carrying a sleeping Nicole off toward the bedroom. A short
while later, he opened the cabin door and softly whistled for
Red. "Come here, girl."

Alicia came with Red.

The light from the cabin was shining behind him, throwing his face in shadow, so Alicia couldn't read his expression. When she finally saw the white flash of his smile, she
knew everything would work out—providing she didn't have
a heart attack first! Her heart was beating like a coffee per-
colator gone mad. "Mind if I sit down?" she asked breathlessly.

"Be my guest."

She wanted to be more than his guest. She wanted to be
the love of his life. But even more than that, she wanted to
be a part of his life. For the time being, she settled for col-
lapsing in the deck chair on his front porch.

Mitch sat in the chair beside her. "If I'd have known that calling Red was the way to get you to come over tonight, I'd have done it a heck of a lot sooner."

"I think we should talk...."

"Wait." He placed his fingers over her lips. "Let me say something first. I know there are times when you don't understand me. And I can't guarantee that there won't be times in the future when you won't feel that way again. But I happen to care about you, princess. Believe it or not."

"I do believe it," she whispered against his fingertips. "But when you shut me out, it hurts."

"I'm sorry." He gently smoothed her hair back from her cheek. "I never meant to hurt you. But I can't change who I am. I don't feel comfortable spilling my guts to somebody."

"Even somebody you care for?"

"Especially somebody I care for, particularly when she hasn't said she cares in return."

"If I didn't care, I wouldn't be here. I'd have given up long ago," she added with a grin.

He smiled in return. "I figured as much."

"Then why did you bring it up?"

"Because it's nice to hear the words."

"That's exactly right. It *is* nice to hear the words. That's why we need to talk this out. Trust me, I know it's hard telling someone else your secrets, talking about your past, about the mistakes you may have made along the way. After thinking about it, I realized I haven't told you that much about my past, either. It's not very fair of me to demand something from you that I'm not willing to do myself. So I'll go first."

"You don't have to tell me anything...."

"I think I do. Otherwise we're going to keep having these arguments." Alicia gave him a condensed version of her relationship with Rob. "He asked me to marry him, but he didn't want me, he just wanted a nanny for his impossible kids. I overheard him talking to a friend of his, and suffice it to say that he made his opinion very clear. He thought I was good for taking care of his kids but not for much else. He'd just sweet-talked me into believing otherwise. So you see, when you suddenly told me about Nicole, I naturally assumed—''

"That I was a bastard, too."

"I was seriously considering marrying the man, Mitch. I should have seen through his act."

"Did you love him?" he asked.

"I thought it was possible that I did," she replied.

"Doesn't sound very definite to me."

"Were you definite about Iris when you met her?" The question popped out of her mouth. "I'm sorry. I'm prying again."

"Don't apologize. You've got a right to know. You have a valid point. It's something we should have talked about before. But my ex-wife is not my favorite topic of conversation, so I avoid talking about her whenever possible."

Alicia placed her hand on top of his. "If it bothers you..."

"Having you misunderstand me bothers me more." Turning his hand, he entwined his fingers with hers. "So here goes. The first time I met Iris, I knew I definitely wanted her. What man wouldn't? You saw her picture. I was young. I had my priorities backasswards. All I saw was her beauty. I never bothered looking any deeper. Unfortunately, I'd already married her before I found out that there's nothing beneath that perfect exterior. Inside there's simply no one home. First and foremost, Iris looks after numero uno. Nothing and no one else is as important to her."

"Not even her daughter?"

"Not even her daughter. Don't get me wrong. Iris isn't a bad mother. She loves Nicole in her own way. She loves her as much as she can love anyone other than herself. It's just that Iris is a woman who's perfected self-centeredness to a fine art."

"Nicole told me she's an art buyer."

"That's right. She specializes in Oriental art. Travels to the Far East twice a year."

"Who looks after Nicole then?" Alicia asked.

"I do, when Iris remembers to tell me when she's leaving. Otherwise, Iris has the housekeeper do it."

Alicia felt an all-too-familiar pang, remembering something Nicole had once said. *I think the daddy bird teaches the babies how to fly, when he's home. Otherwise, the mommy hires someone to do it.*

"There's no need to look so upset," Mitch said, misunderstanding the reason for her expression. "Don't you see that you've got nothing to fear from Iris? You're warm and loving. Fun and generous. You smile and I feel like I've come home."

"That's the nicest thing you've ever said to me," she whispered unsteadily.

"It is? Then I'm definitely falling down on my duties, here."

"No. Don't put it that way, as if it were an obligation you have to fulfill."

"Alicia, look at me." He cupped her chin and turned her face toward him. "I don't say things I don't mean. I may not always say *enough,* but I never say things I don't mean. Got that?"

"Got it," she huskily confirmed.

"Good." He leaned closer to brush his lips over hers.

"Daddy!"

"Coming," he replied. Tugging Alicia to her feet, Mitch brought her with him as he went in to check on his daughter, who was standing in the living room, sleepily brushing her eyes with her fists. "What's the matter, kiddo?" he asked, walking over and scooping her up in his arms.

"I woke up and couldn't get back to sleep."

"I've got a surprise for you. Look who I brought with me."

Alicia smiled hesitantly, noticing that the little girl's formerly ragged haircut had been smoothed out. "Hello, Nicole. I'm sorry I wasn't here earlier to tuck you in. I missed reading to you."

"Did you really?"

"Yes."

"I missed it, too. I fell asleep before Daddy could read me a story before. Can I have a story now?"

Alicia looked to Mitch for guidance.

"All right," he agreed. "Just this once. It's way past your bedtime, you know."

"I want you *both* to read it to me."

As Alicia sat there on Nicole's bed, with the little girl on one side of her and Mitch on the other, she knew her life had somehow reached a turning point and would never be quite the same again. Yet she also knew that Nicole would be returning to her mother in two weeks. Her own return to Minneapolis wasn't all that far off, either.

The look Mitch gave her seemed to say that he, too, knew time was running out, but that their moment *would* come. The way he smiled at her left her in no doubt of that!

"Red wanted to come with me on the airplane to Denver," Nicole was telling Alicia as Mitch loaded his daughter's suitcases into his pickup truck. "But I told her she had to stay here with Daddy so he wouldn't get lonely."

Alicia smiled. "That was very thoughtful of you, Nicole."

"Are you going on an airplane home soon, too?"

"Yes, I am."

"But my daddy's going to stay here, right?"

"As far as I know."

"Just about ready to go, kiddo?" Mitch called out

Alicia knew how hard farewells were on all concerned. In this case, it was all the more poignant because it seemed as if Mitch and Nicole had just reached a special understanding, had just relearned what it really meant to be father and daughter, when it was time to go.

"Will I ever see you again?" Nicole asked Alicia.

"I sure hope so."

"Me, too. I'm gonna miss you."

"Oh, honey, I'm going to miss you," Alicia said. "I'll write to you, though, just like I promised. In fact, I already mailed a letter off to you. It should get there when you do."

"A letter?" Nicole perked up. "Really? I never get mail."

"You will now. And don't forget to look for that surprise in your suitcase when you get home." Alicia had slipped a framed enlargement of the photo she'd taken of Nicole and her father that day at Maligne Lake. The photograph may have lacked the studio perfection of Iris's portrait, and the frame may not have been sterling silver, but it had heart. There was no mistaking the happiness and love glowing from that portrait. She planned on giving a matching one to Mitch.

"I won't forget," Nicole promised.

"We've got to get going, kiddo," Mitch called out.

"Okay." Nicole turned away. Her denim backpack, filled with books, toys, and a bag of Gloria's cookies, was jauntily perched on her back.

Alicia kept her eyes on that backpack as Nicole walked away. She thought Nicole had decided to leave without giving her a hug when the little girl suddenly pivoted and ran back to her.

Alicia dropped to her knees and reached out her arms to engulf Nicole. Tears came to her eyes as Nicole gave her a fierce hug and whispered "I love you!" in her ear. Then, as quickly as she'd come, Nicole was gone, running toward Mitch.

Alicia stood in the driveway with her dad and Gloria to wave them off, staying there long after the truck had disappeared from view.

"Well, they're off," Ray said.

Alicia nodded. Her throat felt too tight for her to speak yet.

Gloria placed a comforting arm around Alicia's shoulders and gave her a hug as gentle as Nicole's had been fierce. "You'll all get together again. I've got no doubt about that."

"I hope you're right."

"I'm always right," Gloria assured her.

When Mitch returned from Edmonton, twilight was just beginning to fall at the lodge. For once, his favorite time of day failed to soothe his soul. The parting at the airport with Nicole had been painful. He felt mangled inside and in need of comfort—in need of Alicia.

She was waiting for him on the lodge's front porch, wearing a red blouse tucked into a full denim skirt and looking like the woman of his dreams. She smelled of flowers and sunshine. Just looking at her helped to ease some of his pain, but none of his frustration.

"How did it go?" she asked softly.

"Not very well. Nicole told me she wished she didn't have to go back."

"What did you say?"

"What could I say? Damn it!" He pounded his fist on the porch railing. "I hate this!"

She ran her hand over his back. "I know it hurts."

"Was it this bad when you were a kid and had to leave to go back to your mom?"

Alicia shrugged. "It wasn't easy. But I knew I'd be back next year and that I'd hear from my dad frequently. He'd call me on the phone, write me, send me pictures of the lodge. Gloria even sent me cookies."

"It was nice of you to write Nicole a letter. I should have thought of that myself. I sent her a postcard from the airport after her plane took off."

"You're a good father, Mitch."

"Yeah, well that remains to be seen."

But Alicia had seen enough to know how much Mitch loved his daughter, how much he cared about her, thought about her. During the past two weeks, he'd gone out of his way to let Nicole know she was loved. Having overheard their touching discussion, Alicia had realized why Mitch felt he needed to spend the extra time with Nicole, and she hadn't begrudged him that.

"Is your dad around?" Mitch asked.

"It seems to be the day for family crises," Alicia noted quietly. "Gloria's sister-in-law called from Vancouver. Gloria's oldest brother had a heart attack. She and my dad left for Edmonton a few hours after you did. They flew to Vancouver so that Gloria could be with her brother for a few days. I told them not to worry about things here, that you and I could hold down the fort."

Mitch nodded, but she could tell he hadn't really registered all the consequences of her announcement. But Alicia had. Aside from the sixty or so guests who were all in their individual cabins, hopefully getting ready to retire for the night, she and Mitch were alone at the lodge tonight.

"I've got some dinner waiting for you, if you're hungry."

Mitch shook his head. "I don't think I could eat."

"Would you rather be alone?" she asked uncertainly.

"No." He took her hand in his. "Come on, let's go for a walk."

Their walk ended up in the living room of his cabin. It was chilly, so Mitch built a fire in the fieldstone fireplace.

Alicia gently removed his hat from his head. "I don't think you'll need this anymore tonight."

Mitch ran a restless hand through his hair, ruffling the dark strands.

"She cried, you know." His voice was harsh. "Once we got to the airport, she cried."

Alicia didn't say anything. She knew there were no words to make him feel better. She could only try to comfort him with her kisses and her love. She began by brushing her lips over the line of his clenched jaw. His skin was warm and slightly rough.

When she reached the corner of his mouth, his restraint disintegrated. Pulling her to him, he kissed her with urgent hunger. *Passion. Desire. Need.* The feelings bombarded Alicia with their powerful intensity. What had started out so softly had exploded into something fiery and volatile, something utterly irresistible. She wrapped her arms around him, needing something solid to hang on to as his lips continued to consume hers.

A moment later, they were both stretched out full length on the native Indian rug in front of the fireplace. Alicia wasn't sure how they'd gotten that way, and she didn't care. She just wanted this moment to continue.

His body posed the question, hers answered—throbbing hardness to soft warmth. No thoughts. No words. Just the erotic friction of the zipper placket of his jeans burning through the soft denim of her skirt. Just the soft swish of him parting her unbuttoned blouse. And excitement. Exhilarating excitement.

Seconds later, he'd unfastened her bra, revealing the alabaster paleness of her breasts to the warmth of firelight and his ardent gaze. There was no time for her to be self-conscious because seconds later, his hands were cupping her with gentle passion. Her breath caught as he lowered his mouth to kiss first one creamy mound and then the other. Her fingers tangled in his hair, holding him to her as he continued to seduce her with his mouth. Then he tempted her with the pointed tip of his tongue and she was completely lost, overwhelmed by the astonishing pleasure.

She arched against him, frustrated by the material still separating them.

Mitch leaned away to stare down at her with fire in his blue eyes. "You better not be doing this because you feel sorry for me," he muttered.

"I'm doing this because I—" she paused, realizing she'd almost admitted her love for him "—because I want to."

"I want to, too. Come on, princess." He stood and tugged her to her feet.

"Where are we going?"

"To bed. Got any objections?"

"No."

"Good."

Nine

They left her blouse in the hallway and his shirt on the doorknob of his bedroom. By the time they reached the bed, her skirt was in a pool around her ankles and her bra had mysteriously disappeared. So had her sandals.

While Mitch perched on the edge of the bed, frantically tugging his boots off, she tempted him by leaning against his bare back and kissing the slope of his shoulders. He stood long enough to shuck his jeans, and then he shoved the bed covers aside and tumbled her onto the sheets. "So you like to tease, do you? Don't give me that innocent look. You know what I'm talking about."

"You mean this?" She brushed against him.

"That's exactly what I mean," he growled.

"You don't like that?"

"Oh, I like it, all right." He trailed his finger down the valley between her breasts. "I just don't want to rush this."

"Me, either." She felt deliciously shy yet wonderfully bold as she followed his cue and traced her fingers over his chest. He was a study of warm flesh and rippling muscles. She counted his ribs, admired the flat plane of his stomach and circled his navel with a teasing fingernail.

"You're playing with dynamite," he warned her.

"Is that what you call it?" The stretchy material of his Jockey shorts left little to her imagination, and her heated look told him so.

"That does it! Prepare to be ravaged!"

He hooked one naked leg across hers and began kissing her with hungry intensity. She soon lost track of where his hands were. Moments later, her white cotton underwear joined his in a heap on the floor. His touch was fleeting but magical as he caressed her body. He brushed his thumb over the peak of her breast and then moved on to the inward curve of her waist.

Her breath caught as his hand moved lower. His touch was unhurried and seductive. Alicia was lifted to a world of luxurious sensations. Her fingers clenched the rumpled sheets, their convulsive opening and closing echoing the pagan rhythm coursing through her lower body—centering in the place where his devilishly adoring fingers were working their magic on her.

She felt so wild and out of control that it scared her. But even more frightening was the thought of stopping this mindless pleasure before it was complete.

Sensing her conflicting thoughts, Mitch brought one of her hands to his body in a silent invitation to enjoy him as he was enjoying her. The instinctive movement of her hands soon had him gasping with excitement. He trembled and then froze as the thrill of her touch became too intense to be borne. He had to move away from her before he lost control.

"I'm sorry," she murmured contritely. "I'm just not very good at this kind of thing yet."

"Honey, you get any better at this and I may die."

She looked encouraged. "Really?"

He nodded and brought her hand back to him. "Just treat me gently," he said with a darkly sexy smile.

She did. For as long as she could. But then the growing need to have him joined with her, filling the aching emptiness, could no longer be denied.

The need was growing within Mitch, as well. "Don't move." Rolling away from her he fumbled for the foil packet in his jeans pocket. He was back a moment later, and she welcomed him with open arms. Unable to wait a second longer, he came to her.

The fit was perfect. Mitch closed his eyes as the pleasure hit him. She was so slick and tight. She was— He paused, having just reached a delicate barrier. She was...a virgin! His eyes flew open to stare at her in surprise. "You're—"

"Dying for you." Her hands were spread across his back as she tugged him down to her. "Come to me. All the way. Please."

With a groan, Mitch discarded his noble intentions and completed their union. He was as gentle as he knew how to be.

For Alicia, the pain was brief, but the satisfaction was infinite as she gathered him in. He was hers now, just as she was his.

"Are you okay?" he whispered, gently smoothing her hair away from her face.

"Fine." She smiled at him. "But I have a feeling you're going to make me feel even better."

"I'll try." Mitch was no expert on virgins. "It's your first time. I'm not sure..."

"I am. Just love me."

He did, seducing her with the rhythmic movement of his body. Alicia's eyes widened, shocked by the unbelievable joy he was creating within her. She'd known there was supposed to be more, but she'd never expected... Was she supposed to feel so wild, so delirious?

"Don't hold back," Mitch said urgently. "It's okay. Go with it...."

She gasped as he rocked against her. Every smooth silky thrust of his hard body produced mystical flutters of ecstasy that grew and took wing... *Incredible!* She breathlessly cried his name.

"That's it, princess." He looked down at her, feeling a primitive satisfaction at the vibrant pleasure reflected on her face. "That's it."

Her fingernails dug into his back as she suddenly shattered into a million pieces, the delicately tensing ripples growing into wave after wave of sheer bliss.

A moment later, Mitch shouted his own release and collapsed in her arms.

It took a while for either of them to regain enough oxygen or energy to speak. And then it was in husky whispers, soft with completion.

"Welcome to my kingdom, princess," he murmured.

"It's *our* kingdom now," she returned with a sultry smile. "And it's called Paradise."

He propped himself up on one elbow. "Are you all right?"

"Perfect."

He gave her a look.

"I am." She ran her hand over the slope of his shoulder. "Stop worrying."

"I can't stop worrying. You should have told me."

His apparent disapproval made her feel uncomfortable. "Look, there's no need for you to be upset about this."

"No?"

"No. I knew what I was doing," she assured him earnestly. "I wanted you to make love to me. I even came prepared." She leaned over to tug a handful of foil packets from the deep pocket of her denim skirt. "I may have been somewhat inexperienced, but I'm not uneducated," she stated with quiet dignity.

"Why?"

She looked at him in confusion. "Why am I not uneducated?"

"No." He took the packets from her hand and set them on the bedside table. "Why were you still inexperienced?"

"Was I that bad?" she asked somewhat stiffly.

"You were incredible." He gave her a heated kiss that was all too brief. "And you gave me no hint that you weren't familiar with intimacy."

"I haven't lived like a nun, you know. I have had relationships in the past. But it never felt right before."

"Why me?" he murmured. "Why give me something that was obviously so important tō you?"

"Because I knew you were the one that I'd been waiting for." He was also the one she loved, but she didn't want to tie him to her that way. "It was meant to be." She shrugged and cranked up the brilliance of her smile. "There's nothing for you to feel guilty about. I'm an adult, and I make my own decisions. I don't regret anything that happened. Not for one second. That doesn't mean you're under any obligation whatsoever."

Mitch placed his hand over her mouth. "Can the fancy talk. I *want* to feel responsible for you."

She tugged his hand away. "Why? Because you're an old-fashioned guy who is feeling guilty about the fact that I just lost my virginity? You didn't take it from me, Mitch," she haughtily informed him. "I gave it to you. Freely. No strings attached."

"What if I want strings? What if I want to feel responsible for you because I'm an old-fashioned guy who happens to love you?"

She eyed him uncertainly. "Is that a rhetorical question?"

"It's my way of saying I love you."

"You do?"

"Why the surprised look? And . . . are you crying?"

Alicia blinked rapidly. "Of course not. You love me?"

The answer was in his eyes, but he answered her aloud anyway. "Yes, I love you. What about you?"

"Well, of course I love you! But I . . ." Her eyes narrowed suspiciously. "You're not just saying you love me out of any sense of obligation, are you?"

"Leave it to a woman to complicate things," he grumbled. "Forget obligation or responsibility. Forget everything but the fact that I love you and that you love me." He tipped her chin up and kissed her. "Think you can do that?"

She nodded, and wrapped her arms around his neck.

"Good." His hand brushed her thigh. "Then just lay back while I have my wicked way with you."

"Again?"

He smiled that slow smile of his. "There are many ways to make love. Let me show you a few. . . ."

Light filtering through the curtains woke Alicia early the next morning. The first thing she saw when she opened her eyes was Mitch staring down at her. "What are you doing?" she asked him sleepily.

"Watching you."

"Why?"

"To make sure I wasn't dreaming."

"I'm real." She took his hand and placed it over her breast. "Don't I feel real?"

"You feel real good," he muttered. "We need to talk."

"You're not going to give me the third degree again, are you?" Her look warned him that she wasn't about to re-hash the subject of her lost virginity again.

"No. I'm not going to question my incredible luck." Placing his hands on either side of her face, he leaned down and kissed her with gentle tenderness. "I've found you and that's enough. When are we going to see each other again?" he murmured in between kisses.

"When...?" Her dreamy-eyed glance shifted to the bedside clock. It was almost six. The realization galvanized her into action. She sat up so quickly she almost knocked Mitch out of bed. "Oh, my gosh! The guests will be up and about soon! I've got to get back to the lodge before anyone comes looking for me."

"You're leaving me already?"

She smiled and smoothed the frown from his forehead. "I'm not going far. The lodge is only about two hundred yards away."

"You may not be going far now, but you will be soon," he noted quietly. "When are you going back to Minneapolis?"

"The middle of next week."

"I've got some vacation time coming. I could fly down to Minneapolis and spend a few days with you, if you want me to."

She lifted his hand to cradle it against her cheek. "I want you to."

Moving her hair to one side, he kissed the vulnerable curve of her neck. "Show me how much you want me to," he murmured suggestively.

"Later." Before he could tempt her further, she jumped out of bed, taking the sheet with her and leaving a disgruntled Mitch behind.

* * *

"This is ridiculous," Mitch muttered as Alicia, fresh from the shower and fully dressed now, opened the door a crack and listened for a sign of anything moving.

"Do you think the coast is clear?" she wondered nervously.

Mitch closed the door and pinned her against it with his half-naked body. "I think I'm going to go crazy not being able to kiss you until tonight."

"Restraint is good for the soul."

"Indulgence is good for the body," he replied, moving against her with suggestive hunger.

"Mmm." She melted in his arms. "Stop tempting me."

"I will if you will."

She ducked under his arm and opened the door. "Hold on to that thought."

"I'd rather hold on to you."

She kissed him. "You will. Soon."

Never had a day seemed so long. Mitch appeared determined to drive her crazy, strutting around in his jeans and white T-shirt with such unabashed sexiness that he made her mouth water. And to make matters worse, he didn't touch her once. Not all day. But then, he didn't have to. He only had to look at her in that certain way and it was as if he were sharing the most intimate of caresses with her.

Alicia fanned herself with a stack of credit-card receipts. As far as she was concerned, nightfall couldn't come quickly enough.

Mitch built another fire that night, in the fireplace and in Alicia's soul. The seduction began on the couch but was soon interrupted by Red—who wanted to join in on the fun.

"She's jealous," Alicia declared with a grin. "She thinks she should be the only one allowed to lick your face."

Mitch groaned. "I'll put her outside."

"Don't do that. It's cold out there."

Red placed her head on the couch cushion two inches from Mitch's nose and gave him one of her woebegone looks.

"Then she can stay in here, but we're leaving." He hustled Alicia up and tugged her after him as he rushed down the hallway to the bedroom. Breathless, they both leaned against the closed door and grinned at each other.

"And they say a dog is a man's best friend," she noted mockingly.

"She got you into my bedroom, didn't she?"

"Oh, so that interruption was planned, was it?"

"Absolutely." He looped his arms around her waist. "Got any complaints about that?"

"None."

"Glad to hear it." He sidestepped her over to the bed. "Aren't you warm in that outfit?"

"Roasting," she murmured.

"Then you better take it off."

"I thought I'd let you do it," she suggested provocatively.

A second later he had her apricot blouse off. Her khaki slacks disappeared next.

Meanwhile, she'd only managed to peel off his white T-shirt. "No fair," she protested breathlessly. "You're getting ahead of me."

"All right, I'll give you a sixty-second head start." He spread out his arms. "Go on."

She did. And she began by pushing him backward onto the bed. The surprised look on his face made the effort well worthwhile.

"I hate to point this out to you, but jeans are much harder to take off when you're lying down," he informed her.

"That's okay," she replied, leaning over him with siren-like seductiveness. "I'll improvise."

Alicia made good on that promise, surprising and delighting him with her creativity.

Any remaining articles of clothing went flying as they came together with awesome speed and incoherent joy. As Alicia held him in her arms afterward, she knew she'd never loved anyone as much as she loved this man.

"Okay, you've convinced me," he murmured against her shoulder. "You can improvise on me anytime you want to."

"You're back already?" Alicia exclaimed when her father and Gloria walked into the lodge late the next afternoon.

"Doesn't sound like you missed us much, pumpkin," Ray noted ruefully.

"Of course I did. How's your brother?" she asked Gloria after hugging her.

"Recovering nicely. It was probably silly of me to go rushing off to be with him like that, but I couldn't help myself. I felt much better after seeing him and talking to the doctors. But there wasn't much I could do for him, so Ray and I decided to come back home. How's everything been here?"

"Fine," Alicia replied. "Everything's been fine."

"No problems?" Ray asked.

"None."

"You and Mitch were able to handle everything, okay?" Gloria inquired.

Alicia nodded, determined not to blush. She was twenty-nine, for heaven's sake, not nineteen. But the memory of what she and Mitch had handled... Hoping to halt her steamy thoughts, she fell back on her old habit of counting to ten in Latin. It didn't help.

"Are those carrot-raisin muffins I smell?" Ray demanded.

"Yes," Alicia quickly replied, welcoming the distraction. "I just made a fresh batch. They're on the kitchen table."

Ray was gone an instant later.

Gloria was slower to take her leave. She gave Alicia a knowing smile and a reassuring pat on her shoulder. "Mitch is a good man," she stated. "You've chosen well."

Dumbstruck, Alicia could only stand there and watch as her stepmother walked away.

"Fasten your seat belts, please. We're about to take off." Alicia did as the flight attendant requested, wondering for the tenth time where the time had gone. Here she was, sitting in the plane, heading back to Minneapolis—leaving her family, her mountains and the love of her life behind. She must be crazy.

She'd certainly had reason to begin doubting her sanity lately. She'd caught herself staring off into space and grinning at nothing more times than she cared to remember. The fact that she'd caught Mitch doing the same thing made her feel a little better. At least she wasn't the only one in seventh heaven.

Two days. In two more days, Mitch would be beginning his vacation by flying to Minneapolis to see her. He was leaving Red with her dad and Gloria. He'd given them permission to use his motorbike, as well. Ray had been delighted with the offer.

Mitch hadn't seen her off at the airport. He'd kissed her goodbye at the lodge, the look in his blue eyes making her promises she couldn't wait for him to keep. Her dad had driven her to Edmonton, just like old times.

Alicia had always left the mountains reluctantly, but this year the tug was particularly strong. Because this year, she'd fallen head-over-heels in love. As the plane rose over the flat

Alberta plains, Alicia looked down, her thoughts on the man she'd left behind.

Once she was back in Minneapolis, Alicia was struck by the overwhelming expanse of sky and the sticky heat. She missed the soothing sound of the river at night. Granted, her second-story apartment was on Lake Calhoun, but it wasn't quite the same thing.

She'd opted for uniqueness and personality in her choice of apartment, preferring the old-fashioned charm of hard-wood floors and huge windows to the starkness of those boxlike modern complexes. Normally, whenever she walked in her front door after time away, she felt a sense of home-coming. Normally...but not today. But then, she hadn't felt normal since meeting Mitch.

Alicia spent the first day airing out her place, sorting through the tons of mostly junk mail that had been held by the post office during her absence, and missing Mitch.

The second day, she refilled her refrigerator, retrieved her plants from her neighbors, and missed Mitch.

By the next day, every flat surface had been dusted and everything else had been vacuumed, including a few things that shouldn't have been—such as her Boston fern. That's what happened when she daydreamed while housecleaning. She ended up mutilating her plants.

She turned the pot the other way and tried consoling her guilt with the observation that this particular fern had needed a haircut anyway.

The knock on her door came sooner than she'd expected. She was still dressed in her cutoffs and tank top. Her hair was piled haphazardly on her head. It couldn't be Mitch! But it was.

"Hi," he said. "I caught an earlier flight."

"Hi. I'm not ready yet," she moaned, tugging the rubber band from her hair and trying to smooth the ruffled strands into place.

"No?" He closed the door behind himself. "I think I can help solve that problem."

"You can?"

He nodded and dropped his bag onto the floor. Gently, he tugged her into his arms and slid his hands down her back until his fingertips rested at the base of her spine. Then he slipped his hands beneath the hem of her tank top, gliding over her bare skin with tempting appreciation. "You're not wearing anything under this."

"I know," she murmured unsteadily.

"I'm glad." He nuzzled her neck. "You smell like lemon."

"It's the furniture polish."

"Aren't you going to kiss me hello?" he whispered a millimeter from her lips.

She not only kissed him *hello,* she kissed him *I love you, I've missed you, I want you, I need you.* Their lips merged with a wildly intense hunger. He kissed her as if he hadn't seen her in months, as if he were starved for her.

"Now do you feel ready?" he whispered in her ear.

"You know how I feel," she whispered back.

"I know." He nipped her earlobe with his strong teeth.

Weak at the knees, she sank to the floor with him, and they made love on her newly vacuumed living-room carpet.

Ten

———

"**T**his is ridiculous," Alicia murmured lazily. "I've got a perfectly good bed right down the hallway."

"We'll try that out later. I don't think I can move yet."

"That's because I'm lying on top of you."

"Clever of you."

"I thought so." She brushed his hair off his forehead, smiling at the pale line of skin that remained untanned because of his hat. "Where's your hat?"

"I left it in Jasper. I feel kind of naked without it."

"You *are* naked."

"Mmm—" he idly stroked the curve of her hip "—so are you."

"Seemed like a good idea at the time."

"Brilliant idea."

"I missed you," she said softly.

"I missed you, too."

Eventually, they did move on to her bedroom. Mitch was surprised to find that unlike her room at the lodge, which had been filled with frills, this room was simple and boldly elegant.

Alicia followed his gaze as it traveled around the room, trying to see it from his point of view. She realized that the white handwoven area rugs were impractical, but she loved them anyway. The purple leather chair and matching ottoman were stunning and had cost her half a month's pay, but were so comfortable that they'd been worth every penny. Besides, they matched one of her prize possessions—an art nouveau figure of a woman with outspread stained-glass wings in muted shades of purple. It sat in a place of honor, atop one of her teak dressers, where the midafternoon light streaming through the window always hit the bits of glass and created chromatic patterns on the white walls. Today was no exception.

This room was her refuge and an expression of that side of her she kept hidden from most people. But not from Mitch.

She watched his lips lift into a smile and saw those familiar crinkling lines appear in his suntanned cheek. "I like it," he stated. "It's you."

He sat down and bounced on her bed, rumpling the purple-and-white comforter. "Soft mattress."

"Get that look out of your eyes," she told him, despite the fact that he looked incredibly sexy sitting there bare-chested. She happened to be wearing his shirt for the moment. "We just abandoned ourselves in the living room barely an hour ago."

"I love it when you talk like a librarian." His arm shot out and an instant later, Alicia found herself on the bed with him. "You sure don't kiss like a librarian."

"And how do you know how a librarian kisses?" she countered suspiciously.

"All right, I confess. You're the only librarian I've ever kissed. These lips—" he brushed his thumb over them "—drive me crazy. I don't know what it is," he mused, going on to trace them with his index finger. "Maybe it's the way your upper lip curves in the middle." Slowly lowering his head, he kissed the corner of her mouth. "Or maybe it's the way you always taste like strawberries," he murmured, his breath ricocheting off her moist mouth. "I always was a sucker for strawberries as a kid. Never could get enough of them. Or of you."

His mouth slanted across hers, ravenously consuming her gasp of pleasure. A tantalizing nibble here, a boldly teasing swirl of his tongue there, and Alicia was burning up.

"Don't worry," he whispered in her ear, "we're not going to abandon ourselves again."

"We're not?"

"Not yet." He tangled his fingers in her hair. "I love the way this feels," he noted, rubbing the strands between his thumb and index finger. "It's as soft as silk. Nothing stiff or sticky." He nuzzled her temple. "And it smells good."

"I-I use honeysuckle shampoo," she said unsteadily.

He smiled. How come he'd never realized how sexy simple scents like lemon and honeysuckle could be? Infinitely better than the cloying heaviness of some designers' hundred-dollar-an-ounce obsessions. "I like it."

Alicia liked it, too—liked...no, *loved* the way he leisurely seduced her with his words and his fingers. His touch was innocent rather than intimate, but the affect was breathtaking. He made her feel beautiful. He made her believe she was beautiful.

"And these hands," he was saying, lifting them to his lips. "These are incredible hands. I have firsthand knowledge of how incredible these hands are."

"Yours are pretty incredible, too." Her voice was soft with desire. "When you touch me, I feel like I'm on fire, like you're touching my soul."

"You feel that way when I touch you?" He trailed a finger down the turned-up curve of her nose, over the luscious curve of her mouth all the way down to the tempting curve of her breast.

"Yes. Oh, yes!"

"I'd touch you even more, but we wouldn't want to abandon ourselves again," he reminded her with a devilish grin.

"We wouldn't?"

"That's what you said."

"I was crazy at the time."

"So you don't want me to stop?"

"Never."

Still he held back, teasing her. "Sure?"

"I'll show you exactly how sure I am." She rolled over until she was perched atop him. "I'm this sure...."

She hovered over him like a sexy angel, kissing her way from his collarbone to his navel. But it was the way she moved against him that blew his mind.

"Where'd you learn how to do that?" he gasped.

An intoxicating smile curved her lips. "I've been reading up, doing my research."

"What else have you learned?"

"Let me show you...." She undid the snap of his jeans.

The lesson in loving was mutually enlightening and blissfully satisfying as Alicia discovered a wanton side of herself that she'd never known existed.

The next few days were filled with further discoveries for Alicia. She took Mitch grocery shopping and found that he loved black olives and couldn't go into a store without buying a can of them. When they went bike riding around the lake one afternoon, Alicia learned that Mitch overwhelmingly preferred horses to ten-speed racing bikes. But the clincher came when Mitch, knowing how much she was enjoying this period of finding out more about him *and* herself, dared her to do something she'd never done before.

"Fine," she agreed. "I know the perfect place."

Mitch looked at her with male anticipation, clearly expecting that perfect place to be somewhere on his body.

"I've never gone to a waterslide before," she took pleasure in informing him. "It's always been on my list of things I'd like to try."

"A waterslide?" He looked as if she'd suggested an elephant trek through Thailand.

"That's right. There's a place just a little south of here that has one. What's the matter?" she inquired, noting his doubtful expression. "Don't cowboys and waterslides go together? You brought a swimsuit, didn't you?"

"Yes, but..."

"Great. I'll go get my suit and we'll be off."

But once she was in the waterslide park's changing room, Alicia began having second thoughts about the wisdom of this idea. She tugged at her blue-and-white-batik print swimsuit, which suddenly seemed much skimpier than she remembered. And had the sweetheart neckline always been so...revealing? Decidedly nervous, she rechecked the fastening of the halter strap. A crowded amusement park was no place for sudden surprises, and this suit had to stay on through what looked like some pretty strenuous maneuvers down the waterslide.

Finally satisfied that everything was as it should be, and unable to put off the moment of reckoning any longer, she left the rest of her belongings in the locker and went to meet Mitch at the snack stand.

She should have guessed that he'd be standing there eating a hot dog. And she should have guessed that he'd look great in a pair of blue swim trunks. The trunks may have been plain, not one of those racy minuscule European models for *her* cowboy, but the man wearing them was very special, indeed.

He looked at ease, sure of himself without being stuck on himself—a rare quality in this age of narcissistic health clubs and tanning salons. *He thinks fast and shoots straight.* Alicia remembered Gloria describing Mitch that way once. She smiled. That was Mitch, all right, an honorable man who just happened to look lean and disturbingly male in plain blue swim trunks.

She watched his eyes as she came closer, loving the way he looked at her. She wasn't real pleased at the way two lissome blondes were looking at him, however.

"This is nice." He ran his finger along the curve of her swimsuit's neckline. "Very nice."

"I'm glad you like it," she said breathlessly. "You look nice, too." Understatement of the decade! "Shall we go?" She wanted him away from those blondes before they started drooling over him.

"Why the hurry?"

"No reason," she fibbed. "Weren't you just about done with that hot dog anyway?"

"Not yet. Want a bite?"

She wrinkled her nose at him and got a kiss for her troubles. He tasted like relish and ketchup. She licked her lips.

"You're right," he muttered. "I think we could use some cold water about now." He dumped the remainder of his hot dog in the trash container. "Let's go."

"Maybe this wasn't such a good idea after all," she said as they ascended the ramp leading to the top of the slide.

"Would you stop saying that?" he grumbled. "You're making me nervous."

"I'm not making you nervous. The drop is making you nervous."

"Look, little kids are doing it. How scary can it be if lit-tle kids are doing it?"

"They don't know any better," she retorted.

"Sure they do. Listen." Mitch tilted his head in the direction of the group of kids ahead of them.

"You get on these bendy kinds of mats and then go zoom," the eight-year-old was telling his friend, who was looking a little green around the gills. "It's the neatest thing."

"There. Doesn't that make you feel better?" Mitch said.

Still undecided, Alicia watched the group sort them-selves out as they prepared to head down on their "bendy kind" of mats. Then they disappeared from view. "Just tell me this," she said with fatalistic resignation. "Is your life insurance paid up?"

"Just get on the mat."

Alicia sat in the front, and Mitch sat behind her, like two children on a sled. His legs bracketed hers. She didn't have time to concentrate on how good his body felt against hers, because an instant later they were flying down the slide.

The first second, Alicia was sure she was heading for cer-tain death. When that hadn't happened by the next second, she thought it might not be so bad after all. The ride was bumpy, exhilarating and faster than she expected. By the time they landed in the pool of water at the bottom, she de-cided she could get to like this.

"Let's do it again!" she exclaimed, wiping the water out of her eyes.

Another devotee came flying down the slide and bumped into her, sending her into Mitch's arms.

"Throwing yourself at me again, are you?" he said with a grin. "It's a little crowded for this sort of thing, don't you think?"

"I think you've got an overactive imagination."

"And it's one of the reasons you like me so well."

"That—" she chased a drop of water as it ran down his cheek toward his mouth "—and the way you look when you're all wet."

"Is this your way of reminding me of that shower we took together last night?"

She clamped her hand over his mouth. "There are children present."

"You're talking like a librarian again," he mumbled against her mouth, before curling his tongue and stroking her palm.

Alicia shivered. She loved this man so much. He touched her soul and rocked her senses. He made her smile. He made her angry at times, but he always made her *feel*. Intensely. Passionately. That he should love her, too, almost seemed too good to be true.

As Mitch paced Alicia's living room early the next morning, he knew their time together was running out. And he knew that his own days of running were also drawing to a close. These past few days with Alicia had taught him one thing: that he had to get his life back in order again. Because he wanted to have a life he could offer to share with her. But before he could do that, he had to go back to Denver, had to face the past and fight those demons. Only then would he be free.

When Alicia woke up, she was alone in bed. Grabbing her purple satin robe, she quickly went looking for Mitch. She found him in the living room, fully dressed and leaning over a stack of papers. To her surprise, he was wearing a pair of round horn-rimmed glasses that made him look more like an accountant than a cowboy or a handyman. Quite a transformation.

Disconcerted, she said, "I didn't know you wore glasses."

There was a great deal she didn't know about him, and Mitch knew this was the time to tell her. Still, he couldn't resist delaying the moment a bit longer as he tugged her onto his lap and kissed her.

Alicia sensed something different about this kiss, and a strange foreboding filled her heart. There was such a desperation tinged with despondency, it almost felt as if he were kissing her goodbye.

She tried to smile into his brooding eyes. "We're going to steam up your glasses," she murmured unsteadily.

He didn't smile as she'd hoped he would. Instead he removed the glasses and tossed them onto her coffee table. Alicia knew then that something was definitely going on, and she had a sinking feeling it wasn't something good.

Since she couldn't think straight sitting on his lap, she moved, curling up onto a nearby chair. "Is something wrong?"

"I've got to go back to Denver."

His blunt announcement caught her by surprise. "Denver?"

He nodded and got to his feet with such restless urgency, she almost expected him to leave right there and then.

Her throat felt frozen, and it took a second or two before she could speak. Even then, her voice was as rusty as an old nail. "Why do you need to go to Denver? To see Nicole?"

"To get my life back in order again. I've been running long enough. It's time I stopped. It's time I faced the past."

"I don't understand." She gripped the chair arm with trembling fingers. "What have you been running from?"

"From the life I left behind in Denver."

Her heart stopped. "You mean your marriage?"

"I mean my construction business. I can't keep expecting my partner to handle the workload by himself."

Alicia began to appreciate what Alice must have felt like while falling down that rabbit hole into Wonderland— completely disoriented. "Your construction business?"

"I haven't been a handyman all my life," he stated irritably.

"I see." She didn't, of course, but the words came out anyway. They were spoken automatically since her brain seemed incapable of functioning for the moment.

"There was an accident," Mitch began jerkily. "A bad one. I was involved. A roof collapsed. We were trapped. Two of my men died. I was a wreck afterward. Couldn't go near a construction site without shaking like a fool. I had to get away. As soon as the divorce papers were signed, I left. Headed north."

The idea of him being in pain distressed her. "How badly were you hurt?" she asked in a shaken voice.

"Physically, I banged up my leg pretty badly. But it was the claustrophobia, the damn shakes, that paralyzed me."

"Oh, Mitch..."

"I didn't tell you this to get your sympathy."

His curtness made her pull back. She should have remembered that he didn't respond well to compassion. Besides, her anger was beginning to simmer as the things he'd told her were slowly starting to sink in. The construction accident, the fact that he co-owned a construction company in Denver, even the glasses—they all added up to a Mitch she didn't know. "Why didn't you tell me any of this before?"

"Because the time wasn't right."

An almost overwhelming sense of déjà vu hit her. Alicia felt the same chill as she had when he'd belatedly told her he had a daughter. The same shock as when she'd discovered that his ex-wife was gorgeous. Now to discover that he wasn't a rambling handyman after all... Alicia dazedly shook her head, trying to clear her thoughts.

She'd thought the landscape of his life had been cleared of land mines, but here she'd stumbled over yet another one. How many more were there out there waiting to explode in her face? What else was he keeping from her, waiting until he felt that the time was "right"?

Feeling the need for some distance, Alicia moved away from him and stood with her back to him as she stared out the window.

"Aren't you going to say anything?" he demanded after the silence had stretched on and on.

She shrugged. "What's there to say?"

"I expected you to get angry, yell, shout, something."

"What good would that do? You're going to do whatever you want to do regardless of what I say or think about it."

"That's not true," he denied.

She turned to give him a challenging look. "Isn't it?"

"No."

"You told me you were going back to Denver. You didn't ask me or consult with me. You *told* me. That doesn't leave much room for discussion."

"You're twisting my words around again."

"All I know is *what* you choose to tell me, *when* you choose to tell me."

"You're blowing this way out of proportion."

"Am I? Fine. Then we'll just forget about it. Drop the subject. Unless you'd care to tell me when you plan on leaving for Denver?"

"Early this afternoon."

Alicia barely held back a gasp of startled pain and betrayal. She'd thought they'd have at least another day together. "Nice of you to let me know ahead of time," she said in a strangled voice. "I suppose I should be glad you didn't just leave a note on my pillow saying 'Thanks, it's been fun. Gotta go.'"

"I'll be back."

"Sure you will," she noted cynically.

"I mean it."

"Right."

"For a woman who claims to love me, it doesn't sound like you have much faith in me," he stated angrily.

"Do you blame me?"

"Yes. I've never given you reason not to trust me!"

"Excuse me if I disagree with you. Withholding the truth from me is certainly cause for distrust."

"You're making this much harder than it has to be," he growled.

"Right! Try and put the blame on me! That's just great! *You're* the one who doesn't tell me about his daughter, or his beautiful ex-wife, or about an entirely different life you apparently led in Denver, yet *I'm* the one at fault? Isn't that just like a man!"

"And how like a woman to get hysterical over nothing!" he shot back.

"Nothing?" she sputtered angrily. "You pretended to be something you're not!"

"I wasn't pretending."

Another thought occurred to her. "Does my dad know that you're not planning on going back to Jasper?"

"No. I didn't know myself until last night."

"What about Red? Are you just going to desert her, too?"

"I'm not deserting anybody," he shouted. "I'm just trying to get my life back in order! Is that so much to ask?"

"Far be it from me to get in your way," she said stiffly. "I'll help you pack."

"Wait a minute." He caught her arm as she stalked past him. "I didn't mean that the way it sounded."

She pulled away from him. "I know what you meant. You've got places to go, things to do." Places and things that had nothing to do with her, Alicia thought in despair.

An hour later, Mitch was packed, his single bag set by the door. A cab waited for him downstairs. And by the closed look on Alicia's face, he knew she was no closer to believing him now than she had been before.

"You know," he said darkly, "maybe I'm not the only one who has some facing up to do."

"What's that supposed to mean?"

"That maybe it's time you faced a few fears of your own. Like the fear that I don't really love you, that you're not pretty enough to love, that I must have some ulterior motive for loving you. I must need a mother figure for my daughter, or I must be attracted to you because you're so unlike my ex-wife. Or the latest accusation, that I must be using you for a quick lay. Loving someone means trusting him."

"Exactly. And did you trust me when you didn't tell me about Nicole or about your past?"

"Is this your way of repaying me for that?"

"No!" Alicia bit back the tears. How could they have been so close and still misunderstand each other so greatly? It felt as if there were a gulf between them as wide as the Grand Canyon. "You'd better go. You'll miss your flight."

"I'll be back."

"Don't make promises you can't keep."

He glared at her. "I'll be back."

Then he was gone.

Eleven

Alicia hurt too badly to cry. In the past, she'd been accused of being a softy who got misty-eyed over the opening bars of the *1812 Overture*. Yet here she was, dry-eyed despite the fact that her heart was breaking.

It was crazy. She was crazy. The world was crazy.

She was on edge, her emotions as vulnerable as fresh paint. Unable to face the memories of Mitch—the rumpled pillow where he'd slept, the couch where they'd argued—she hurriedly changed clothes and left her apartment. For some reason she got the brilliant idea of going jogging around the lake, even though she hadn't jogged since the previous year. She ended up with a charley horse in her leg. The memories, however, were still with her.

Throughout the rest of that day her eyes prickled as if the tears were about to start. But they never came. Neither did a call from Mitch.

Alicia had held out some misplaced hope that he'd phone her once he'd arrived in Denver. Silly of her. No doubt he was already totally wrapped up in his old life, a life that included a beautiful ex-wife. Did Iris have anything to do with his return to Denver? Was he with her now? The possibility tormented Alicia. But still she couldn't cry.

Needing to keep busy, she cleaned out her closet, determined not to think about anything. The resulting chaos was not encouraging.

When Alicia started work the next day, she deliberately wore one of her favorite outfits, a rayon pant suit in royal blue. The kids didn't come in until the following day, so Alicia spent most of her day setting up bulletin board displays. Her heart stopped when she came across some decorations for the four basic food groups.

Isn't ice cream one of the five basic food groups? She heard Mitch's voice so clearly that she looked over her shoulder, half-expecting him to be standing there. He wasn't—but her friend, teacher Pam Muehler, was.

The disappointment overwhelmed Alicia as she dropped the decorations back into the box. That particular display would have to wait. She couldn't face it now.

"It's only the first day back, and already someone's trying to ban a book from the library," Pam was saying as she perched on the corner of Alicia's desk. "The parents of one of my new students sent me a note suggesting I speak to the librarian about the literary standards of *The Wizard of Oz*. I'm really looking forward to parent-teacher conferences with these folks, let me tell you."

"That's nice," Alicia murmured absently.

"Banning books is nice?"

"I'm sorry," Alicia apologized. "I guess my mind wandered for a minute there."

"Thinking about those gorgeous mountains of yours, I'll bet. I envy you going up to the Canadian Rockies each summer. I got your postcard, by the way. Is it really as spectacular as it looks up there?''

Alicia nodded.

"You're real talkative today," Pam noted with a teasing smile.

I'm suffering from a broken heart. What do you expect? Alicia wanted to say. But she didn't. Her hell-on-wheels days seemed far behind her now. Yet the pain of Mitch's departure remained as fresh as the moment he'd walked out her door.

The tears finally did come later that night, when she was watching one of those sentimental phone-company commercials, of all things. Once started, her crying jag continued through most of the night. She used up an entire box of Kleenex.

If any of her co-workers noticed her red-rimmed eyes the next morning, they were kind enough not to make any comment. The children in Mrs. Ivanhoe's first-grade class were not as generous.

"You look funny."

"My mom's eyes looked like that when my dad bought our new car."

"My sister's eyes look like that when she swims in the pool."

"When my eyes looked like that, they made me stay home from school."

I should be so lucky, Alicia thought with a grimace.

The phone was ringing when she got home from work that evening. Thinking it might be Mitch, Alicia let the grocery bag drop to the floor as she dove for the phone.

"Hello?"

"Pumpkin, is that you?" Ray asked. "You sound so out of breath. Everything okay?"

"I just walked in the door," Alicia replied, thereby avoiding his question about being okay. "Uh, you haven't heard from Mitch by any chance, have you, Dad?"

"As a matter of fact, I have. Just got a call from him a short while ago. He's in Denver, you know."

"I know."

"Did he call you, too?"

"No. He mentioned something earlier about returning to Denver." And to Iris? a voice tormented her. "How did he sound?"

"He sounded fine."

"Did he say how long he'd be staying in Denver?"

"No. He did quit, though. Said he'd let us know when he'd be coming up to Jasper to gather his belongings and Red, of course."

"He quit!" The news was enough to make the tears start flowing again.

"There's no reason to cry, honey. We can get another handyman, no problem."

"Let me talk to her," Alicia heard Gloria say in the background.

"Still think I've chosen well?" Alicia asked unsteadily.

"You two had another fight," Gloria guessed.

"He's not really a handyman, after all. He owns part of a construction company in Denver."

"So he just told us."

"Can you believe that? And now he leaves you and Dad in the lurch."

"It's not as bad as all that. Actually, we've already hired a replacement."

As far as she was concerned, Alicia knew she'd never be able to find a replacement for Mitch. She tossed a wadded-up damp Kleenex into the garbage can, wishing she could dump her feelings for Mitch as easily.

"Alicia, are you still there?" Gloria anxiously asked.

"Yes."

"What did Mitch actually say to you?"

"That he'd be back," she admitted.

"Then what's the problem?"

"The problem is that I don't believe him. How can I, when he keeps the truth from me? He doles out information about himself as if it were gold, measuring out miserly little bits at a time!"

"But you love him anyway."

"I know. What's wrong with me?" Alicia wailed.

"Nothing's wrong with you."

"Then why can't I be sure that Mitch loves me?"

"I don't know. How can anyone be sure that someone loves them? There is no test, unfortunately. You have to trust your instincts, your heart."

"Were you sure that Dad loved you when you married him?" Alicia asked.

"I was sure I loved him, that I could live with him, that I could bear to wash his underwear, that I could listen to his voice and his jokes for the rest of my life. Was I sure he loved me? No. I believed he loved me. Certainty takes time. Do you believe Mitch loves you?"

"Sometimes."

"You know, your father and I could have gone through the same period of doubt—was he marrying me to get a mother for his children? Was I marrying him for his money?"

"Why didn't you have those doubts?"

"Because of a handy little thing called faith. Not blind faith that can't tell right from wrong, but twenty-twenty faith. The kind that says 'I know who you are. I know your strengths and your weaknesses. I'll believe in you if you'll believe in me.' Granted, Mitch may have kept things from you, and that was wrong of him, but has he ever said something and not followed through on it?"

"No."

"I didn't think so. In our experience with him, Mitch has always kept his word."

Gloria's comment triggered a memory in Alicia's mind as Mitch's words came back to her. *I don't say things I don't mean. I may not always say enough, but I never say things I don't mean.*

"Maybe it's my own judgement I'm doubting, not Mitch," Alicia murmured with a flash of insight. Thinking about it, she realized that was true. After her experience with Rob, she hadn't trusted her ability to make the right decision. "Damn it!" she exclaimed, startling Gloria on the other end of the phone line. "I'm not going to let that piece of cow dung ruin my life any further!"

"Mitch?"

"Of course not. Rob! I thought I'd gotten rid of all the bad baggage from that relationship. But there was one last item left. Before he left, Mitch told me that it was time I faced a few fears of my own. I guess he was right."

It was so clear to her now. There was no comparing Rob to Mitch. Rob's meaningless smooth talk could have applied to anyone. But what had Mitch said that he'd loved about her? Generalities? Things she knew not to be true? No. He'd said he loved her enthusiasm, the joy she got out of life, the curve of her lips, the feel of her hair. Small things. Unique things that applied only to her.

And wasn't that why she loved him? Because of all the small things, the unique things—his determination, his old-fashioned sense of honor, the way his eyes crinkled at the corners whenever he smiled, his Donald Duck impersonation and the fact that he kept a battered four-leaf clover in his wallet.

I'll believe in you if you'll believe in me, she wanted to tell him. Mitch hadn't stopped believing in her, and she refused to stop believing in him. He said he'd be back—that meant he'd be back. As soon as he could. He'd be back. She knew it. She just had to be patient.

Never had a week seemed so long to Alicia, not even when she'd been five waiting for Christmas to come, or thirteen and had poison ivy, or twenty-five and waiting for her job to come through. It had been six days and two hours since Mitch had left, not that she was counting. No, she was keeping busy, placing and misplacing library book orders among other things. Her desk looked like a paper war had been declared and she'd lost. Which seemed only fitting since she felt lost without Mitch.

"Ms. Donnelly." Someone tugged at her skirt. "You were going to help me find a book. I want one on riddles."

You want riddles, try to figure out male-female relationships, Alicia thought to herself.

"Or on dogs," the first-grader added.

"One dog book coming up," Alicia said.

The next half hour was hectic as she tried to find the right book for each of the thirty first-graders. Then she checked the books out to them, writing down the first name and last initial of those whose printing left something to be desired.

She was in the midst of printing "Demetrius O." when out of the general low-level babble she heard one of the children say "Who's that?"

She looked up, and there was Mitch standing in the library doorway, looking exhausted but looking so damn good that she just stood there staring at him, praying that she wasn't hallucinating. Did hallucinations breathe? Did they have blue eyes that gleamed with hope and determination? This one did.

Alicia drew in a shaky breath. He was real, and he even had a new Stetson hat that he kept turning in his hands.

"It's a cowboy!" one of the boys shrieked with excitement.

"It's not Halloween yet," one of his classmates pointed out. "What's a cowboy doing here?"

"Where do you think he left his horse?" another wondered.

"Cowboys use helicopters now," someone else claimed. "I saw it on TV."

The class bombarded Mitch with questions, but he didn't even hear them. He should have called first, but he'd wanted everything finished before speaking to Alicia. Now he drank in the sight of her. She was wearing a skirt . . . red. And her blouse was white with little red numbers on it. Had she been wearing the most exclusive designer's evening dress, she couldn't have looked better to him than she did at that moment.

Alicia moved from behind the library's small circulation desk, accompanied by a chattering group of children. She walked toward him slowly.

She took one step.

He took two.

Their hands met, fingertips first, then palms. A touch became a grasp as they twined fingers with a strength of purpose that no one could break. With all the children surrounding them, they couldn't do more than merely hold hands, but it was enough as they each mouthed the words the other was waiting to hear—"I love you."

Later, in the privacy of Alicia's apartment, the explanations came. They were once again sharing the living room couch, sitting close together. Mitch had his arm around Alicia's shoulder as she rested her cheek on his chest.

Part of her wanted to hug him for coming back to her, and part of her wanted to sock him one for leaving her in the first place. She compromised by tightening her arms around his waist. "Why didn't you call me?" she asked.

"I should have, I know. It's just that I thought it would be better to explain in person. And then I was trying to get everything done as quickly as possible so I could come back here to you."

She traced the lines grooved in his cheek. "You look tired."

"So do you." He turned his head in order to kiss her fingers. "I've got so much to tell you. It turns out that Tom, he's my partner, wants to buy out my half of the business. He hadn't offered to do that before in case I wanted to come back. Once I got there, I realized that I could handle being back. And that was enough for me. I'm not saying the claustrophobia is gone, but the shakes were. I was able to function again. That's partly thanks to you."

"Me? What did I do?"

"Loved me. Called me on things I did wrong. Made me deal with my problems. I could have stayed at the construction company. But I didn't want to. This time I left out of choice, not out of necessity, not because I'd been driven away by the bad memories. I told Tom I'd take him up on his offer to buy my half. Then I went to see Iris."

Alicia stiffened. She couldn't help herself.

Mitch immediately felt the change. "What?"

"Nothing." She relaxed against him, telling herself she couldn't get all tense each time he mentioned his ex-wife's name. "Go on."

"We talked about Nicole and the fact that she's not happy. Outside of school, which is one of those snobby private deals, Nicole doesn't get a chance to mix with friends her own age because Iris doesn't like having a bunch of screaming kids around. I told Iris what Nicole had said to me, about not wanting a family—"

"—because kids just get in the way?"

He gave her a surprised look. "Yeah. How did you know?"

"I was standing on your porch at the time and over-heard. It wasn't intentional."

"Yeah, well, when I told Iris about it, she actually looked upset. For the first time in years, we talked, really talked, about Nicole. We didn't argue. We didn't fight. We just talked. And in the end, she agreed to give me joint custody of Nicole."

"Oh, Mitch, that's wonderful! I'm so glad for you."

"There's more. I plan on bringing Nicole to live with me here in Minneapolis. There are several houses for sale in your neighborhood. I thought I might buy one and reno-vate it. What with selling my share of the company, I've got enough money to sit back for a while. And enough to put down on a house—that blue one on the corner, for in-stance. But I wanted you to see it before I made any final decisions."

"You want my architectural advice?"

"I want you to marry me." The words were no sooner out than Mitch was muttering, "Damn it! I was going to pro-pose properly, take you out to dinner, roses, the whole thing. Now I've blown it."

"Yes."

"What?"

"Yes, I want to marry you."

"You do?"

"Yes."

"Despite the fact that I have a daughter and an Irish set-ter?"

"Don't forget the battered pickup truck and the four-leaf clover in your wallet. Yes, despite all that and because of it."

He smiled.

So did she.

This was the moment they'd been waiting for. Slowly, deliberately, Mitch lowered his lips to hers. They'd kissed before, in the car on the way home and again on their arrival at her apartment, but this kiss was the culmination of their love and commitment.

"When?" he murmured against her mouth.

"When what?" she whispered back.

"When can we get married?"

"When are you bringing Nicole and Red to Minneapolis?"

"As soon as possible." He kissed the luscious curve of her upper lip. "I thought I'd fly back to Jasper, pick up Red and the rest of my stuff and then drive the pickup down to Denver to get Nicole." He brushed a finger over her bottom lip. "If you like the house, then I'll buy it before I leave for Jasper."

"How about a Valentine's Day wedding?"

"Halloween's closer."

"New Year's Eve?" she suggested.

"Thanksgiving."

She grinned. "How about Groundhog Day?"

"We'll discuss this later," he decided, silencing her with a kiss. "You're obviously not in the proper mood now." He kissed her again, groaning as her lips parted and clung to his with sweet abandon. "Mmm, you're definitely in an *improper* mood. Time for bed."

"But it's not even five o'clock," she laughingly protested as he hurried her toward the bedroom.

"That late, eh?" He unbuttoned her blouse, kissing every inch of skin he uncovered. "Amazing how time flies when you're having fun."

As Alicia sank onto the bed with him, she knew she'd be having fun with this man for the rest of her life—and she was looking forward to every minute of it!

Epilogue

Edmonton International Airport, the following June

"These your bags?"

Alicia smiled at the man's curt question. But a moment later her smile disappeared as he took off with her suitcases.

"Hey, you! Come back with those!" Alicia called out.

When the man stopped, she gently chided him. "I told you I'm only three months pregnant. There's no reason I can't carry the small bag myself."

But Mitch, her husband of six months, stubbornly held on to the bags. "Yes, there is."

"Look, there are Grandpa Ray and Grandma Gloria!" Nicole exclaimed. "You better not let them see you fighting or you're gonna get in trouble."

"Thanks for the warning, kiddo. But it's too late. I'm already in trouble," Mitch murmured for Alicia's ears only.

"And I have been since the moment you sicced that policeman on me a year ago."

It seemed only fitting, since the man who'd walked into
her life by walking off with her suitcases had also walked off
with her heart. She wouldn't have it any other way!

* * * * *

Silhouette Desire

COMING NEXT MONTH

NIGHT LIGHT
Jennifer Greene

On a dark and windy night, Bree Reynaud knocked
on the door of Simon Courtland's recently inherited
spooky mansion, never expecting that he'd turn up
in her bedroom later as a half-clad sleepwalker!

FEVER PITCH
Sherryl Woods

Cassie Miles was through with sportsmen! They
might have nice bodies but they nearly always liked
to play the field. Was Jake Starr really any different?

WOMAN TAMER
Barbara McCauley

Garrett Williams was an egotistical womanizer who
had written a book telling men how to handle the
modern female. Denelle Thompson decided that
she was going to show him just how wrong he was.

Silhouette Desire

COMING NEXT MONTH

OUTLAW
Elizabeth Lowell

This is the first book in Elizabeth Lowell's
WESTERN LOVERS series; it tells the story of
rough-and-tough Tennesee Blackthorn, July's _Man
of the Month._ To win his lady Ten was going to have
to prove that he could be tender as well as tough.

IN A MARRYING MOOD
Raye Morgan

Cam Sterling was back in town, and he was every
inch as gorgeous as Ann remembered. Not that he'd
ever noticed her. Now Cam — still charming — was
looking for a wife and Cam in a marrying mood was
irresistible!

MAVERICK HEART
Jackie Merritt

Rugged rancher Bart Scanlon couldn't believe that
Torey Lancaster hadn't known that when they were
children he'd had a crush on her. Even now, she was
special…